# DEATH BEATS
# THE BAND

# DEATH BEATS THE BAND

## Ida Shurman

COACHWHIP PUBLICATIONS

Greenville, Ohio

*To My Parents*

*Death Beats the Band*, by Ida Shurman
© 2021 Coachwhip Publications edition

Front cover: Stan Kenton Orchestra, William P. Gottlieb / Ira and Leonore S. Gershwin Fund Collection, Music Division, Library of Congress

First published 1943
Ida Shurman Frankel, 1916-1997, graduated from Hunter College and the Juilliard School of Music. When this novel was published in 1943, she was working as a Junior Professional Assistant in radio physics at Fort Monmouth. She married Dr. Jesse J. Frankel, sociologist.
CoachwhipBooks.com

ISBN 1-61646-505-0
ISBN-13 978-1-61646-505-6

# 1

Jack Coler was feeling highly elated as he guided his Plymouth sedan along the brightly lit Jersey state road. He was hunched down in his seat, his long legs comfortably sprawled out under the wheel, and his orange-red hair burning out from the upturned collar of his coat. The highway stretched before him, empty and lonely, and beyond the fence of brightness formed by the radiation of the road lights, the countryside loomed dark and deserted in the cold winter night. Still, Jack felt that exhilarating sensation one gets from champagne bubbles tickling the nostrils. He was sitting on top of the whole darn world!

He glanced at his companion sitting silent and preoccupied beside him. "What's the matter, Windy? Tired?" he asked.

"Nah!" came the reply. "I was just getting kind of worried about the weather. Get a load of that wind! Sure sounds vicious out. We're gonna have one of those blizzards tonight that we'll be boring our grandkids with in fifty years. I don't like it at all. Can't you speed 'er up a little?"

Jack peered through the windshield. Windy was right. There certainly was trouble brewing outdoors. The heavy wind was beginning to make driving troublesome.

"Is it much further?" he asked, bearing down on the gas pedal.

"About twenty more minutes ride," answered Windy. "Slow down now. You turn left right here."

Jack swung the wheel sharply, and turned the car onto a bumpy, badly lit dirt road. "How do customers ever find their way to the Log House?" he asked, as he piloted the car with difficulty. "Looks like they hid it away on purpose."

"Don't worry, they find it. Max Harris knows his business. He gives them good food, good liquor, and good dance music—an unbeatable combination—and he usually has a full house. You know the old gag about building a better mouse trap. Only it doesn't look like there'll be any mice there tonight, not with that lulu ready to break. Oh, well, it's no money out of my pocket. Say, you act as though you're up in a cloud. What is it—your first job?"

"Yes, it is," answered Jack, trying to be nonchalant about it. "That is, it will be, if my bass fiddle survives those bumps. Gosh! Imagine me playing bass with Andy Parker, no less! Andy Parker—world-famous bandleader, trombonist, singer, songwriter—"

"—and louse," Windy finished for him. "With a capital *L!*"

"What do you mean, louse? I thought he was supposed to be such a swell guy. What's wrong with him?"

"Well, to tell the truth, I don't know exactly," Windy admitted. "This happens to be my first job with him too. Only from what I've heard from guys who've played with him that schmaltzy build-up is strictly a press agent's dream. I don't know anything definite against him, you understand, just that he's hard to get along with. Acts like he was Crosby, Gershwin, and Toscanini rolled into one. I dunno, though. He's probably O.K. if you get on the right side of him. As long as his pay checks don't bounce, it's all right with me."

Jack digested this information in silence. "Well, anyway," he burst out defensively, "you must admit that his latest song, *Headlined in My Heart,* hit the jackpot. That measure in the middle, where he sings the vocal, and you hear the sax trio playing that snazzy obbligato against the melody—say, that's clear out of this world!"

"That's true," agreed Windy. "You gotta hand it to him. At least he's a good musician. That is the best song he's written so far. Nice color in the harmony. Say, how come you got a job with Andy right off the bat like that? Someone recommend you?"

"Yes, Louie Carter."

"The colored bass player? No kidding!" Windy was properly impressed. "No wonder Music Agents, Incorporated sent you down tonight without an audition."

A sudden thump interrupted the conversation.

"Hey!" cried Jack, slowing down momentarily. "I think my fiddle and your sax are getting chummy, Windy." Windy turned around and peered into the dim interior of the car. He saw his clarinet case on the floor. His saxophone was still on the back seat where he had put it, and Jack's bull fiddle had slipped down on its side against the door. Their suitcases had slid around, but were in no danger of turning upside down.

"It's O.K., Jack. The instruments are still whole, but just take it easy now. We're almost there. What were you saying about Louie Carter?"

"Well, it was this way: I got my B.B.A. degree at N.Y.U. a few years ago, and I had just about decided that I didn't care for business administration when both my parents were killed in an automobile accident."

"Gosh!" exclaimed Windy, his voice gruff with sympathy. "That's rotten!"

"Well—" Jack tried to be matter of fact—"it wasn't very pleasant. I was in the back seat, and I saw the whole thing—escaped with a cut on my chin. I'm an only child, and—well, my folks were— Oh, what's the use? . . . Coming that way, I collapsed. A nervous breakdown, the doctor said. He suggested that I do something—something I liked—to occupy my mind. He thought studying music might help. My dad left enough money so that I didn't have to worry about making a living, for a while, anyway. I'd studied the violin when I was a kid, and I went to work seriously on the whole works: orchestration, theory, harmony, and all the rest of it. I studied with Louie, and since his instrument was the bass, I concentrated on that for my instrument too."

"You sure picked yourself a teacher. Doghouse Carter, no less! He's good enough for me, any time. Andy sure won't kick either."

"I hope not," said Jack a little doubtfully.

"Sounds like some life," Windy added enviously. "Nothing to do except study and play around at playing. Not bad."

"It wasn't as wonderful as it sounds. You get tired of loafing after a while. I wanted to make some money of my own, just to prove I wasn't utterly useless. I didn't think I was good enough to play with a decent band yet, so I started looking around for some kind of job. I had no practical experience in anything, so it seemed hopeless. Then, a couple of weeks ago, I saw an ad in the 'Help Wanted' column that sounded exciting. It asked for a college graduate, experience unnecessary, for work of a confidential nature. I fitted the bill, so I answered the ad. It turned out to be a job in a private detective agency. You know those tabloid stories about divorce cases: 'Mr. Pastrami discovered in an apartment with an unidentified, undressed blonde by Mrs. Pastrami and two witnesses. . . .' Well, I was one of the witnesses. Talk about dirty work—smoking out the cuckoos from their love nests takes the cake of soap! I was just about ready to quit anyway, when Louie gave me a ring this morning, and said this job was open for me if I wanted it. Imagine—if *I* wanted a job with Andy Parker? Louie encouraged me to think I was ready for it, so I went down to the agency and told them he'd sent me down. So ends my short career as a detective, thank goodness!"

"Well, Louie ought to know about your ability as a musician," Windy reassured him.

"How about you, Windy?" Jack asked. "I've read about you in *Metronome* and *Downbeat*. And I bought that last waxing you made for Columbia on *Fascinating Rhythm*. Practically wore it out, too. That clarinet of yours almost talks in the second chorus."

Windy chuckled a little self-consciously. "You never know where you find a fan, eh?"

"I've often wondered why you didn't start a band of your own."

"Takes too much money, and even if you have enough, it's a toss-up. I can always get a good job with a name band, and that gives me security of a sort."

"How come you're willing to play third sax with Andy Parker?" Jack asked curiously. "You won't be getting much opportunity for clarinet solos with him."

"Well," Windy replied, "I got fed up with my last job a couple of months ago. That was in Chicago. So I quit and came east. I loafed around a couple of months, just taking a rest, and making a few recordings. Then, today, Music Agents offered me my choice of a berth with Glenn Miller, or this job with Andy Parker. I tossed a coin, and Andy won—or maybe he lost, depending on how you look at it."

"Oh, don't be so modest," protested Jack. "Only I think you're nuts for not going with Glenn Miller. Gosh—I'd give an arm to play with him."

"Maybe you're right," Windy acknowledged. "But he's going on tour now for a while, mostly playing one-night stands. Otherwise I'd have gone with him. Andy is stationed at the Log House Casino for a time, and I'd like to sleep in the same bed twice in succession for a change. Guess I'm getting old."

Old? Jack turned his attention momentarily from the troublesome road ahead, and gave his companion a hasty scrutiny. He saw a likable-looking young man, with a round face which appeared rounder because of the hat brim pulled down over it. He had the smooth, transparent skin of a baby, and a small bulb of a nose. With the full, small mouth, and the suggestion of a double chin, the rimless glasses he wore made him look more or less like a studious cherub. His coat collar, like Jack's, was pulled high around his face, scant protection against the cold.

"I'm going to be thirty next month," volunteered Windy, submitting to Jack's scrutiny with a cheerful grin. "Don't laugh—that's old for a swing musician. They need glamor boys nowadays. When you start losing your hair, you're finished."

"Thanks for the tip," laughed Jack. "From now on it's nightly massage for me."

"Watch out—you'll burn yourself," teased Windy, eyeing Jack's thick, red, hatless thatch. "And incidentally, talking about thanks, thank you for the lift. It's lucky I met you at the agency, or else I'd never have made it out here."

"That's all right. Don't mention it," answered Jack. "I'm glad to have your company on this long ride. Besides, I don't think I'd have found the place without your help, especially in this awful weather."

They rode on in silence, the bumpy road taking their breath away, until Windy, who had been peering anxiously through the window, suddenly exclaimed, "Cripes! That snowstorm's caught up with us! And here we are, still out in the cold, cru-el woild. Hope we don't get stranded out here in the wilds of Jersey."

"Don't worry, Windy," replied Jack a trifle absently. "This car is sturdy, and practically fool-proof." The windshield was spotted white now, and though he had turned on the wipers, they didn't seem to be of much help. It looked as though ice were going to coat it soon.

Jack gave his complete attention to his driving, which was becoming increasingly difficult. The snow was whirling about them in frenzied white flakes. He could see them against the beam of his headlights, but unfortunately, that was about all he could see. The twin rays of light barely penetrated the muddy gray cloud ahead. The wind pushed furiously and heavily against the car.

"I hope we're not late, Windy," he said suddenly. "It must be after eight by now, and we should have been there. I'd hate to get off on the wrong foot on my first night with the band."

"Don't give it a second thought," answered Windy cheerfully. "The band probably won't start playing till after ten. As a matter of fact, we'll be lucky if there's anyone there to play for. There won't be more than a few people tonight, what with this storm. The Log House Casino is sure going to lose on its investment in Andy tonight. We should worry about it, though, as long as we get paid. And by Max the money is good. He's a square guy."

"Max Harris—he's the owner of the Log House, isn't he? You seem to know him," said Jack, his eyes on the blank white wall ahead.

"Yeah. I played at his joint before with another band. Hallelujah! Here we are, thank God! I didn't think we'd make it."

"Whew! Just in time," said Jack as he turned into the driveway against the wind. The wheel seemed like a live thing in his hands, and the windshield was banked with ice. It would have been suicide to go further.

He drove into a parking space which was practically empty except for a few scattered cars. Jack could see dimly through the gloom a low rambling building that seemed to be made of real logs, and was gaily decorated with colored lights that made only pastel spots in the stormy darkness. Beyond, a larger building, also made of enormous logs, was but dimly visible. The two buildings were connected by a structure after the fashion of Siamese twins.

"That larger building is the Log House proper, a hotel," volunteered Windy, as they removed their suitcases and instruments from the back of the car. "The smaller one is the Log House Casino. Max runs it altogether separately from the hotel. There are rooms for the musicians over the Casino."

Jack peered at it for a moment while the wind howled threateningly around him; then he locked the car hastily, and they started making their way to the door. The sting-ing particles of ice and the violent wind made headway difficult, especially since Jack was carrying a huge bull fiddle, and he gave a huge sigh of relief when they reached the entrance.

"Zowie!" he exclaimed, as Windy opened the door. "Watch me curl up near a radiator, snuggled around a hot water bottle." The door opened into a large foyer. On one side was the check room, and on the opposite side was a door, slightly ajar, and bearing the legend:

PRIVATE—KEEP OUT
THIS MEANS YOU

and in between was an opening through which Jack could see a stretch of smoothly waxed flooring, evidently the Casino proper. Off to one side was an entrance to the bar.

As they put down their suitcases, the thumps resounded in the foyer. Jack smacked his frozen hands together, the fingers stiff in their gloves. At the sounds, the door with the request for privacy opened quickly, and a bald ball of a man rolled toward them.

"Come right in," his voice squeaked cordially. "Come in. Glad to see you. Terrible out, isn't it? . . ." Just then his eyes lit on the instrument cases in their individual, incipient puddles. "Oh!" His tone became markedly less cordial. "Musicians!"

Windy grinned at him, as he unbuttoned his overcoat. "Hi, Max, you fat son-of-a-gun! Same old Sourpuss, aren't you? Whatsamatter, don't you recognize me?"

"Oh, it's you, Windy." Max's attitude became a little less frigid. "What the devil are *you* doing here? Not going to play with Andy, are you?"

"Yep. Why—what's up?" asked Windy, winking at Jack. "Has he been giving you trouble?"

"Trouble!" snorted the little man, the iron-gray fringes around his head quivering in indignation. "Don't ask! The headaches that good-for-nothing gives me. Why didn't I stick to the hotel business? No—" his tirade became increasingly bitter—"I had to branch out with a dance hall with name bands! And of all the name bands in the United States, I had to get stuck with Andy Parker! A five months contract I had to sign with him! And ever since he's been here, I've had trouble that Hitler should only have!"

"Easy there, Max," Windy interrupted soothingly. "You'll bust a pipe if you aren't careful. I'm sure Andy isn't that bad. O.K., so he's a stinker. So what can you do, as long as he brings in the customers? And he does, doesn't he?"

Max subsided slowly, still spluttering. "So what? Is money everything?" He gazed solemnly at Jack, and Windy took the hint.

"This is Jack Coler, Max. He's the bass player. Jack, this is Max Harris."

Max shook hands soberly, looking up at Jack's six feet, two inches of lean height. "Pleased to meetcha, Jack. I hope you like it here." Then he suddenly emitted one of his characteristic snorts, and burst out vehemently with "Hmph! Fat chance!" Then he was recalled to his duties as host.

"Oops, here I am keeping you guys with my troubles. You must be frozen. Come, I'll take you up to your room, so you can change into your tuxes. The rest of the band is already in the lounge. But God knows who you're gonna play for tonight," he muttered gloomily as he led the way in, followed by Jack and Windy carrying their paraphernalia. Jack didn't have much chance to see what the place looked like as they entered the dance hall. He was too busy manipulating his big fiddle. They walked about halfway through the hall, then turned to an exit in the right wall, which led to a staircase. As they ascended, Max continued expounding pessimistically:

"There's maybe four, maybe five couples here tonight. Just a bunch of kids. What a night for business!"

"Oh, stop complaining, Max," Windy interrupted with a smile, his clear skin flushed red by his exertions. "You know you didn't expect anyone in weather like this. You know enough about business to make allowances for setbacks. You'll pack the place in another night, and make up for it."

"I suppose so," Max admitted grudgingly. "Well, fellers, here y'are." And he opened a door at the end of the corridor. "You two room together, and you share a bathroom with two other musicians. There's one bathroom for every two bedrooms. Not bad for a log cabin, eh?" he concluded with pride.

Jack had to stoop as he entered the room behind Max and Windy. His tall, thin figure looked like a jackknife folding up. Then he straightened up, and examined the room. It was small, but adequate, and was simply furnished in maplewood. It contained twin beds with a table between them, two straight-backed chairs, two comfortable arm chairs, and two dressers. It was pleasant, and Jack looked gratefully at the radiator in the corner, which was merrily hissing steam.

"Oh, Max," said Windy as he put his coat down, "I forgot to ask about Kitty. How's the little apple of your eye? She must be quite a looker by now."

The apparently innocent question started Max off again. "Kitty!" he snorted, "It's lucky her mother ain't alive to see what's going on. That no-good! Why can't he leave my daughter alone? She's still just a kid. What's eighteen years for a girl now? Hasn't that stick-waver enough women without her?"

Max walked out, still muttering; then he popped his bald head in through the door, announcing sullenly: "I'll tell him you're here," and closed it again.

"Hm!" said Jack. "So Andy's making a play for Max's kid. The plot sickens, eh?"

Windy put his grip on the chair, and started unpacking. "Yeah, that's how it goes," he said casually. "Andy's supposed to be poison for women. Seems they just can't resist him. Too bad for Kitty if he's got his eye on her, though. She's a little flighty, but a nice kid. Max's whole life is wrapped up in her, so Andy had better be careful how he behaves."

# 2

Freshly shaved and dressed, the two musicians were ready to go down about twenty minutes later. On the way out, Jack stopped in front of the mirror for one last look at himself. His long, lanky figure had to stoop over so that he could see his face, with its white, freckled skin, the light-lashed, blue eyes that gave him a perpetually somnolent look, and that scar on his jawline, sole reminder of the accident that had been so costly. He saw only the bright freckles, and the unruly red hair that dimmed everything by contrast, and he completed his self-survey, disheartened by what he thought was his unattractive appearance. He had no idea of the charm contained in his sudden, broad smile which revealed perfect white teeth. He made one last attempt to straighten his black bow tie, then straightened up, deciding he was as presentable as possible.

Windy had been watching him. Putting his hand suggestively on his hip, he snickered in a falsetto: "You look simp-ul-ly bee-oot-ee-full, Jackie, dear—except for maybe just a shade more lipstick. Whoo-*whoo!*"

"Oh, can it, Windy!" Jack's face flushed to match his hair, and the scar on his chin stood out lividly against the red of his skin. "Come on; let's get going." He picked up his bull fiddle, its canvas cover still slightly damp, Windy took his two instruments, and they descended the stairs.

They entered the empty dance hall, and as they approached the raised bandstand directly opposite the entrance to the Casino, Jack looked about him with interest, taking in all the details.

The rustic motif was evident throughout the interior, as well as the exterior. In addition to the usual tables covered with checkered tablecloths, there were also small private dining booths at regular intervals along the side walls, all resembling miniature log cabins. A number of stuffed moose heads and tanned deer hides lined the walls, and on the bandstand, Jack could see the music stands lined up in groups before the instrument racks. As he came closer, it became apparent that the music stands were half-circular, and were made of something that looked like rough bark. On each one were the large sized letters A P made of twigs. As he walked up the few steps leading directly to the bandstand, on the left, he saw that the voluminous curtains covering the back wall were made of rough sacking, and had Andy Parker's name sprawled across them in large letters.

Jack was so busy taking everything in that, before he knew it, he had tripped over one of the instrument stands in his way, and was rewarded with a painful blow on the shin. He put down his fiddle hastily, and bent down to rub the tender spot. At the same time he let loose with several juicy and succinct epithets. He was really waxing eloquent, when Windy grabbed his arm and muttered:

"Shut up, you dope! Where d'ya think you are?"

Jack looked behind him, and to his horror saw heads popping out here and there from the individual cabins.

"Holy cat!" he blurted, his face a symphony in scarlet. "I thought all the cabins were empty. Why the devil didn't you warn me?"

"No harm done," said Windy, laughing at Jack's discomfiture. "That always happens to newcomers here. Now you're initiated." And he pushed aside the curtains, disclosing a door.

Jack felt a wave of anticipation rise within him as he and Windy entered the lounge. It was a large, brightly lit room, hazy with cigarette smoke, and was nicely though simply furnished. Against the left wall was a spinet piano, at which a long-limbed, dark-haired boy was playing some fancy variations on *Chopsticks*. Next to him, a swarthy young man was sitting on a straight-backed chair with a saxophone between his knees, cleaning and testing the instrument. There was a door in the wall directly opposite, leading outside, and near it was a group of three card players around a bridge table. On his right, Jack saw a long table piled high with music and magazines, and at it a medium-sized fellow with horn-rimmed spectacles was sorting music parts, while right next to him a combination radio and record player was blaring out an Andy Parker recording of *Left Alone Blues*. Nearby, a solidly built person was napping in an arm chair, his face covered by an opened copy of *Esquire*.

It all looked very cozy, except that in the center of the room, Max was evidently in the midst of an argument with an individual whose face looked vaguely familiar. Jack recognized him suddenly as Andy Parker. Andy Parker was a name to conjure with in musical circles. Jack found it difficult to reconcile the great name of Andy Parker with this rather dissipated individual, with heavily pomaded, honey-colored hair in rigid waves wearing thin at the temples. The weary-lidded eyes had much more than a suggestion of bags under them, and he had a thin-bridged nose with flaring nostrils; an infinitesimal mustache over thin, red, discontented lips; and a weak chin. He was supposed to be in the neighborhood of thirty, but he looked nearer forty. "Boy," thought Jack in his disappointment, "those photographers sure did some heavy retouching on those pictures he releases for publicity." So this disagreeable-looking, undersized character in the powder blue evening jacket with wine tie was the great Andy Parker!

Max's shrill voice, now becoming louder, could now be heard more clearly against the counterpoint of *Chopsticks* and the trombone wailing coming from the phonograph:

". . . And I'm warning you—you won't have a chance to bother her much longer!" His voices rose a half-octave. "My Kitty is a good girl, and you can't fool around with her without being responsible to me for it, you—you no good musician, you!"

"Oh, go lay an egg, you old hen!" Andy interrupted insolently as he lit a cigarette. He clicked the lighter shut and expelled a mouthful of smoke ceilingward with a contemptuous air of indifference. Then he noticed the newcomers who were still standing in the doorway.

"So you finally got here!" he said, obviously glad of the interruption. "What do you mean by walking in so late? Oh, well, come on in and meet the boys."

The various members of the group continued what they were doing with no more than brief, incurious glances at the two; all but the *Chopstick* enthusiast, who swung into a funeral march and muttered: "Welcome to the arena, Christians. The lion awaits!"

Jack hesitated, then stepped forward toward the bandleader and held out his hand, saying: "I'm Coler, bull fiddle. Glad to meet you, Mr. Parker."

Andy ignored Jack's outstretched hand, and put his own hands in his pockets, while his cigarette dangled from the corner of his mouth.

"Coler, eh?" he asked, raising his eyebrows superciliously. "Which one are you—Coca, or Pepsi?"

"Heh, heh!" a thin-faced youngster at the card table ridiculed. "Get a load of Parker, the poor man's Bob Hope!"

"Shut up, Buddy!" snapped Andy, his eyes glittering with sudden rage.

"He thought for a half hour, then quick as a flash, he shot back the retort perfect: 'Shut up!'" mimicked Buddy, calmly picking up the cards dealt him. "Just a fugitive from the 'Bright Sayings' column."

"The first name's Jack," interposed Jack hastily, "and this is Windy Carmichael."

"Oh, yes, our new sax player." Andy seemed to have recovered at least partially from his anger. "I've heard about you. Tops on the clarinet, eh? Well, glad to have you with us."

Buddy dropped his cards and stood up, stretching. His wide, sharp mouth, pointed chin, and oddly slanting eyes made him look strangely like a malicious leprechaun. He was slim, and looked barely twenty.

"I'll do the honors for you, Andy," he offered, grinning impudently. "That'll save you the trouble of dirtying your mouth speaking to, or of, us.

"I'm Buddy O'Connor, first trumpet with this alleged band. Also the bane of Andy's existence." He made a grandiose bow, and strolled over to the spinet.

"This gentleman at the piano," he continued, "is Iggy Hughes, our best musician, bar none!" The glance he gave Andy was significant, and Andy turned his back on him. "As you may have guessed, Iggy is our pianist."

Iggy stood up from the stool, and flashed a smiling "H'ya?" at the newcomers. He was fairly tall, just under six feet, with the build to carry his height off gracefully. He had black, curly hair, and great, dark eyes rimmed with unnaturally long black lashes. He reminded Jack of a collar ad illustration, and the illusion was heightened by the fact that the planes of his slim, chiseled face were sharply defined by the clean, sweeping lines. "Gosh, he's handsome!" thought Jack a little enviously. "Probably has a rotten disposition, and is as conceited as hell," he consoled himself. Then his natural honesty compelled him to admit that even though there was a moody expression about the mouth, Iggy appeared to be as good-natured as he was handsome.

Buddy had passed on to the saxophone-cleaner. "This—er—person is Tony Carezzi, our tenor sax. Want any throats cut? Tony'll do it for you cheerfully—for a stipend, of course. His theme song is *Who Will Buy My Violence?*"

Tony acknowledged the introduction with a faint curl at the outer edge of his upper lip. The category in which Buddy had filed him appeared to bother him not at all. He was swarthy and oily-looking, with red lips that had a perpetually moist look, and a bluish outline on his skin of the type that makes a man look in constant need of a shave. His shiny, patent-leather hair added to his Latin appearance. He went right back to his work after the barely civil acknowledgment of Buddy's introduction.

"And this," continued Buddy, nodding toward the young man occupied with the music at the table, "is Ray Burns—has the first alto sax seat. Pretty good, too." Ray's thick-lensed, horn-rimmed glasses gave him a rather scholarly look. His only outstanding feature was a sharp, beaklike nose. Otherwise, he was the type that would pass unnoticed in almost any group—of medium height, medium build, and neither dark nor fair. He shook hands calmly and silently with Jack and Windy, then turned casually back to his music.

"Next on our list," said Buddy, going to the card table and indicating one of the players, "is our second trumpeter. Take it from me, Jimmy, here, blows a mean cornet." Jimmy smiled at them. He was pleasant-looking, and appeared almost as young as Buddy did.

"And this is Frankie Jannings, our drummer," Buddy indicated the last member of the card-playing trio. Frankie, a nervous tic in his beady eyes which were slightly too close together, nodded unsmilingly. He had a hooked nose, and bony, angular features, with a receding chin that did its unsuccessful best to obscure the prominent Adam's apple. The narrow forehead and shaggy hair that needed cutting badly gave him an unprepossessing look.

"Well," said Buddy, scratching his head, "that's the lot of us—such as we are. Oops! Almost forgot about Si." He ambled over to the figure in the chair. "Tsk, tsk!" Buddy shook his head in disparagement as he contemplated the half full whiskey bottle on the table nearby. He whisked the magazine off the face, and they saw a fair, broad-faced young man with thick, straw-colored hair falling over his flushed face. His eyes were tightly closed, and his breathing was audible.

"This," said Buddy, raising his pointed eyebrows, "when it isn't drunk, is our guitarist, Si Corey."

"Did that — — — pass out again?" Andy scowled with rage as he eyed the recumbent, oblivious figure. "That's the second time this week! He won't be able to play tonight either." Andy let loose with another violent string of epithets, and concluded: "Just for that, I'm gonna dock him a week's pay, and if it happens again, he's fired!"

"Again?" asked Buddy innocently.

"That's another one of those things that shortens a bandleader's life!" Andy raged on. "What a bunch of slobs!" He turned to Windy and Jack. "I hope you two'll be better. At least I'll have a good musician in you, Windy. You won't be hitting those sour notes like that sax player I had to fire last night."

"You fired *him?* Why, Elmer!" drawled Buddy, his arms akimbo. "That ain't the way *I* heerd it!" His voice took on a chiding expression. "Let's get it straight for the benefit of our new additions. We don't want them to get the wrong impression, do we? It seems that after one of the usual arguments with you, Joe resigned—said you were coming out of his ears; and then his brother, Corky, said that that went for him too; and so the two of them just upped and quit, and they lived happily ever after. Which left you with a bass and sax missing."

Buddy then turned to Jack and Windy. "Don't worry, you two. He never fires a player unless the guy absolutely smells. The boys in our bunch have stayed the longest of any he's had so far, and we've been with him about six months, all the ones that are left, that is. It's too damn hard for him to get decent musicians to stay with him, isn't it, Maestro dear?" he concluded, turning to Andy.

Andy's face turned the color of an over-ripe eggplant. He was about to explode, but before he could say anything, Frankie interposed sullenly, while his Adam's apple moved up and down spasmodically: "Lay off him, Buddy! What good does it do to get him mad? He's unpleasant enough as it is."

"Mind your own business, you—you trap-happy drummer!" Andy whirled on him, his rage finding an outlet. "Who asked you? I can take care of myself!"

"Su-u-re you can!" Buddy drawled in a syrupy voice, enjoying the baiting hugely. "Sure you can take care of yourself. How about defending your honor on the field of battle at dawn? Choose your own weapons. What'll it be, Sweetheart—cream puffs at thirty paces?"

"Speaking of players who smell," sneered Andy, controlling himself with an obvious effort, "not that I wanna mention any names, you understand, but it seems to me that a certain horn player whose initials are Buddy O'Connor has been smelling plenty lately. The kind of corn you've been giving out with belongs in Iowa for the pigs out there, and not with a decent band. Believe me, it's strictly from hunger!"

"Is that so?" asked Buddy, tight-lipped, his eyes narrowing. "Is that the only way you can get back at me—by criticizing my playing? Why, you crumby old has-been, I play better than you ever dreamed of playing, and you know it only too damn well!"

"You don't say!" Andy apparently thought he had acquired the verbal mastery over Buddy. "Seems to me it was you who hit that clinker at rehearsal this afternoon, or maybe it was the man in the moon joining in the jam session."

"I did *not* hit a clinker, but I am going to hit a *stinker!*" shouted Buddy, and started for Andy with his fists clenched.

"Boys, boys!" pleaded Max, rushing into the breach, and almost getting knocked out for his trouble. "Please, boys, stop it, please. . . ." But the others had already intervened and separated them. Buddy sat down again at the card table and Andy straightened his tie, biting angrily at his lower lip.

Max sank moaning into an overstuffed chair, his feet barely reaching the floor. "Oh, God!" he commiserated unhappily. "Fights and arguments, fights and arguments, all the time, all the time! What did I do that I should be punished like this? Bands I needed! Music I had to have! Headaches I got instead, only headaches! If I needed music so bad, I should have bought me a juke box! No musicians, no trouble, and it would have been a million times cheaper. No—I gotta spend extra fortunes buying three network wires a week yet, just to make that schlemiel famous!"

"Make *me* famous? Oh, can the hot air, fat boy!" Andy shrugged his shoulders, and pushed the hair back off his forehead with a graceful, studied motion. "You don't have to do me any favors," he continued. "I was plenty famous before you signed me up for your smelly, fifth-rate joint. My style is a byword all over the country."

"You bet!" laughed the irrepressible Buddy. *"Everybody's* heard of Andy Parker and his Makes-Ya-Wanna-Puke Music!"

"Shut *up!"* yelled Andy, livid with fury.

"And just look at all the crowds waiting to storm the Casino just for the sight of Andy," continued Buddy, ignoring Andy with infinite contempt. He turned to Max. "You should have had a real drawing card, Max. Something like Bingo, or even free dishes for the ladies. Then you would have packed the place in, storm or no storm."

Andy could contain himself no longer, and let loose with a string of lurid curses that left no portion of Buddy's ancestry or character untouched. Suddenly, in the midst of a more violent burst of oratory, the pianist brought his hands down on the piano keys in a crashing discord that startled the entire room, including Andy, into silence.

"Pass me my hat, boys," he said, his black eyes bitter. "I think this is where I came in."

Just then, they heard a light knock on the door. Remembering afterward, Jack was quite sure he had heard only two light raps, but he realized later that it was only because he had been so stupidly deaf. Two light raps? Oh, no! It was really the clang of a fire bell; it was the da-da-da-DUM of Beethoven's Sixth; it was the last high, loud and hot note of a trumpet; it was the pounding of a million hearts beating in unison; and it was only the pounding of Jack's heart when the door opened, on a vision . . .

# 3

The vision entered—a heavenly, out-of-this-world vision, in a white, misty dress, with a glittery red girdle around an unbelievably tiny waist; a vision with cloudy, blue-black hair sweeping her shoulders, with smoky gray eyes, a gardenia skin, and firm red lips; a vision that was the whole world's dream girl.

The vision spoke, and, wonder of wonders, she had a voice to match her looks, low and infinitely sweet. (A technicolored dream with sound effects!) Jack noticed then that she had a worried little frown on her smooth forehead, but even that was becoming. Then he paid attention to what she was saying.

". . . And I think there's something wrong with the phone in your office, Max, because just as Dad was beginning to tell me more explicitly what the doctor said about Mother, the phone started buzzing like mad, and Dad's voice came through very dimly. We both shouted into the receivers, and then we were suddenly cut off completely. Perhaps you can tell what's wrong?"

Max shook his head despairingly. "Everything happens to me! I didn't have enough trouble—now the phone has to break down!" His face suddenly brightened, and he continued: "Maybe it's just my office phone that's out of order. The phone in the kitchen may still be working; that one or one of the pay booths. I'll go see, Lee." And he scurried out.

Lee! So this was Lee Sheridan, Andy's vocalist. Lee, who in the few months since she had been with the band, had made a wonderful reputation for herself in the business. She had just won a magazine competition as the leading female vocalist, a coveted honor. Jack had listened constantly to Andy's frequent broadcasts to hear her sing. Her style was fresh, direct and individual, and scorned the saccharine glissandos of the run-of-the-mill vocalists. She seemed destined to go far: her own program, sponsors, and eventually Hollywood. Hadn't he read something about her in one of Winchell's columns just last week? The exact nature of the item eluded him at the moment, so he contented himself with watching her, and hoping that one of the boys would introduce them quickly. But no one seemed to think of it.

The pianist had walked over to her, his long legs covering the short distance between them in a few steps. He looked concerned. "Exactly what did your dad say about your mother before you were cut off, Lee?" he asked. "Isn't she getting any better?"

Lee's slim hand went up to her forehead in a weary motion. She seemed to have difficulty in answering, and when she finally did so, her voice hinted at suppressed tears.

"He was just telling me that the doctor suggested an operation—that it might help, although they couldn't say for sure. It's just a chance for her . . . Oh, I don't know—" She stopped, with a hopeless shrug of her lovely shoulders, and turned away.

Iggy put an arm about her, his dark eyes luminous with sympathy. "If there's anything—anything at all I can do, Lee," he said gently, "you know—"

"Thanks, Iggy," she said, smiling up at him. "But what can you possibly do? You're sweet to offer, though."

Andy, who had been filing his nails, broke in with a bored grimace: "Go ahead, Iggy, and make with the *Hearts and Flowers*, why don't you?"

Iggy gave him a black look, but said nothing.

"All this gab is just a waste of time," continued Andy. "Come on and let's get going. You two'll have to do without rehearsal—" he nodded at Jack and Windy—"just for tonight, but it won't matter so much. Can't be helped, anyway. Let's see, now—" He got up, walked over to the table, and consulted a printed sheet on it.

"Our first set will start off with a fast number; make it *Bye, Bye, Blues,* the instrumental version. Buddy gets the second chorus solo on that, and remember—no clinkers!"

Buddy wrinkled his nose in derision, but wonder of wonders, he remained silent.

Andy pursed his lips, then continued: "I think *Stormy Weather'll* fit in O.K. after that. There's your vocal in this set, Lee. And make sure you get away from the mike as soon as you're through, because I come in right there with a trombone break."

"Don't worry," Lee said, giving him a long, level look filled with contempt. "I'll try my best not to let anyone see me there. Perhaps it would be still better if I sang from behind a screen? Then I wouldn't detract *any* attention from you."

"Never mind the wisecracks," Andy growled. "Just attend to what I pay you for. After *Stormy Weather,* we'll do *Booglie-Wooglie Piggy.* The band has a vocal interpolation on that number. It's written out in the manuscript, so you two newcomers'll catch on if you aren't lamebrains.

"After that tune," he continued, scanning the sheet, "we'll do *Headlined in My Heart . . .*"

"Inevitably," murmured Buddy, with an incomprehensible glance at Iggy, who was back at the piano.

"I do my vocal on that," continued Andy, with a warning scowl at Buddy. "I'd better explain to you two that I do this one with the bandstand in complete darkness, except for a spotlight on me . . ."

"Andy is never afraid of being conspicuous," interrupted Buddy with a puckish wink at Jack.

"Shut your trap, Buddy," snapped Andy impatiently. "To continue, you two'll be able to read your parts, because when the overhead lights go out, there are flashlights built right into the music stands, and they light up automatically. They're not noticeable from out front, and the entire bandstand remains dark. I don't think you'll have any trouble."

"We'll get along O.K.," Windy volunteered, looking bored.

"Fine! Then we finish up with that nifty new arrangement of *Blue Skies* that we rehearsed this afternoon. I'll tell you the set-up of the next set after we're through playing this one. Ray, you dig out the orchestrations, and hand out the parts. And make it snappy!"

Ray looked imperturbable, and took his time about following Andy's bidding. Andy was about to let loose another stream of denunciation, but at a bland look from Ray, he seemed to change his mind.

But Jack was no longer interested in Andy. Lee had walked out after the bandleader's directions, and without any volition on his part, Jack followed her. It was almost as if something physical had bound him to her.

Lee paused just outside the door. She smiled at him, and said: "Hello, there. I suppose you're one of the emergency replacements. Which one are you—bass or sax?"

Jack stood there and looked at her, somehow unable to answer immediately. His heart was beating eight to the bar, tattooing a message to his brain: "Go on, stupid; what are you waiting for? Hurry up and tell her how unbelievably wonderful she is. Tell her she's a lovely April day—a Jerome Kern melody—a Tommy Dorsey solo . . . Tell her she's everything you've ever dreamed about. Well, what are you waiting for?"

"Oh shut up!" he answered his heart. "You sound like a rotten imitation of *You're the Top.*"

Although his mouth seemed to be filled with a bale and a half of cotton, Jack suddenly, to his great horror, heard himself saying: "Gosh, Miss Sheridan, you're—you're beautiful!"

A dimple Shirley-Templed into the corner of her mouth. Then she said gravely: "I could hang things on that line if it weren't so worn. You might at least try being original."

"But it isn't a line!" Jack denied vehemently. "You've got to believe me. I'm not much good at saying pretty things to girls, but I thought how beautiful you were, and before I knew it I was telling you what I thought. I didn't mean to be fresh, or anything like that."

She smiled at his earnest expression, and said: "Explanation accepted. And incidentally, we don't stand much on formality around here, so you might just as well start calling me Lee now." And she extended her hand toward him.

"My name's Jack—Jack Coler. I'm the bass player."

"Hello, Jack." They shook hands solemnly; then they laughed together. Lee looked up and down his long length with satisfaction. "I'm certainly glad to see a good-sized bass player," she said. "Lately it seems as though only the pee-wees have been playing the bull fiddle. They look funny plucking away at that outsize instrument."

"I'm glad you approve of my height," he answered, as he looked down at her. "Now I wouldn't shrink for anything in the world." Then he continued more seriously:

"I'm sorry to hear that your mother is ill. I hope everything will come out all right."

"Thank you, Jack," she answered, her face clouding again. "I hope so too."

"And—and that other fellow—" Jack hesitated, "I think Buddy called him Iggy—"

"Yes, Iggy. It's short for Ignace, as in Paderewski—just a nickname the boys have given him because he plays the piano so well. What about him?"

"Is he—er—I mean—are you two—er—do you—?" Jack stumbled desperately.

Lee gave him a sidelong glance from her wide gray eyes. "Iggy and I are very good friends, but nothing else, if that's what you mean," she answered. "You see, he's carrying the torch for a Gal What Done Him Wrong."

"That's too bad," sympathized Jack, trying hard to keep from grinning his relief. "He seems like a swell guy."

"He is!" Lee assured him, entirely too warmly, thought Jack. "He's really the grandest person."

"And—and is there—I mean—" Then Jack plunged boldly in: "You're not attached to anyone else, are you?"

That tantalizing dimple appeared again. "Nary a soul. You certainly believe in the direct approach. Don't waste a minute, do you?"

"No, why should I?" Jack could hardly believe his ears. Here he was, conversing with this heavenly creature as though he had always known her. Come to think of it, that was exactly how he felt. Perhaps they had known each other in some previous incarnation . . .

"Incidentally," she said, breaking into his complacent reflections, "that other newcomer looks rather familiar. Who is he?"

"You mean Windy Carmichael? He's the well-known clarinetist. He's doubling on the sax here. You've probably seen his picture in one of the trade magazines."

"I suppose so," Lee said, wrinkling her nose in an utterly charming manner, making Jack's heart skip a beat. "I was just wondering. He's rather nice-looking, isn't he?"

Windy nice-looking? Jack thought about it, then decided in relief that Windy wasn't the type he had to worry about as a possible rival. The handsome pianist was the one to keep an eye on, Lee's denials to the contrary.

"Windy's a swell egg," Jack agreed hastily, "I picked him up at the agency and drove down with him. But why waste time on him? Let's talk about you."

"All right, my public," she laughed. "What would you like to know?"

"Let me see. First of all, how do you like singing for your supper?"

Lee hesitated. "I like singing, naturally. But frankly, I'd prefer to be singing somewhere else."

"I see what you mean," Jack said, nodding his understanding. "Just one big scrappy family, eh?"

"Oh, no!" Lee denied earnestly. "The boys are grand; that is, they would be if Andy just gave them the chance to be. He's so irritating, and downright rotten. He doesn't miss any opportunity to hurt us, so naturally, they try to get back at him in every possible way. Those wisecracks, for instance. I suppose you've already had a sample of that?"

"And how!" Jack agreed. "Buddy doesn't pull any punches."

"Buddy doesn't mean any harm. He's just a kid. But all those things get under Andy's skin, and he gets nastier and nastier, and so on, far into the night. It's just a vicious circle."

"And you do mean vicious!" Jack concluded for her.

Lee shook her head despairingly. Her eyebrows, winging off her forehead, drew together to form a worried line. "You know, Jack," she said, "sometimes I wonder where it'll all end."

"There's always friction in any group that works together so incessantly," Jack assured her. "Especially with temperamental musicians. You're just being over-imaginative."

"No, I'm not," she denied. "It's more serious than you think. You haven't been with Andy for months like the rest of us. You don't know how rotten he can be."

"Maybe so," agreed Jack, smiling indulgently at her, "but I certainly have to give him credit for knowing how to pick his vocalists."

"Oh-oh!" Lee gave him an exaggeratedly arch glance, fluttering her long black lashes. "Here we go again, boys!"

"No, Lee, I really mean it seriously. I'm not just trying to flatter you. You do sing beautifully. And, if you remember, so did the vocalist that Andy had before you. What was her name, anyway? It's right on the tip of my tongue . . ."

"You mean Rosanne Abbott?" Lee's face assumed a guarded look, and her lashes hid her eyes.

"That's the one. Boy, can she swing a mean tune! I haven't heard her for a while, though. Do you know with what band she's singing now?"

"She's dead!" Lee said flatly. "Committed suicide two months ago."

"No!" Jack exclaimed, aghast. "But why? She had talent and looks and personality. She was on her way up! She had everything to live for, so why—?"

Lee turned away. "We'd better stop this gossiping," she said coldly. "I still have to fix my hair, and if you don't go in and get your bass parts, Andy'll hit the ceiling." And before Jack could reply, she had walked quickly across the floor, and had disappeared behind the curtain on the other side.

Jack stood there and watched her retreating back. Then he scratched his red head with a worried gesture. "She certainly marched away in a huff," he thought, completely at sea. "And just when she seemed to like me. I wonder what I said to make her mad? Must have been something about that Abbott girl, but what was it? Women—oh, nuts!" And he returned disconsolately to the lounge.

Just then, Max scurried up the few steps to the bandstand, and came through the doorway with Jack.

"The wires must have blown down," he announced breathlessly to the room at large, as he shut the door behind him. "None of the phones work at all. So what'll we do now?"

"What do you expect to do?" snapped Andy irritably. "By the time we need a phone, the company will probably have repaired the wires. And even if they haven't, they could hear your big mouth all the way to New York without a phone.

"Say, you!" he continued, addressing Jack. "Who told you to wander off? Didn't you hear me say that all of you were to get your parts? That went for you too! And besides, I don't want any of my hired help alley-catting around this joint. Not that you'll get anywhere hanging around Lady Brenda Nose-in-the-Air, anyhow!" he concluded, his voice ugly.

Jack felt the blood rush to his face in anger. He understood now the attitude of the rest of the band toward this—this cheap imitation of Napoleon. He clenched his fists grimly, but Windy, noticing his determined expression, poked him and whispered:

"Easy there, kid. Here are your bass parts. I collected them for you."

"Thanks, Windy," he answered mechanically, "You're a pal."

"Must you guys stand around and chin all day?" Andy was in his normal stride, and still going strong. "We're playing tonight, you know, not for tomorrow's breakfast!"

Tony, now finished with his sax, picked up the instrument as if to give it one last test, and blew out something that sounded like the first cousin to a raspberry. Andy eyed him suspiciously, but the saxophonist looked right back at him with bland innocence spread across his swarthy face.

"Guess my sax is O.K. now," he said and, walking over to the window, peered through the Venetian blind.

"Tsk-tsk!" he continued. "What a storm! That wind is practically tearing the chimneys from your joint, Max." He turned around and smiled, his white teeth flashing wickedly. "Just the kind of night when Andy would dispossess his unconventional daughter with an inconvenient baby—if he had a daughter, if she had a baby."

Andy flashed him a look filled with meaning. "Go easy on the wisecracks, Tony, if you know what's good for you." His tone was threatening out of all proportion to the incident. "I'm warning you, be careful!"

Tony stifled a retort, but his glance at Andy was filled with unconcealed venom.

This meaningless exchange that appeared to be fraught with significance bewildered Jack. What was going on here, anyway. Was it possible that Lee had been right in her apprehensions?

Andy walked over to the armchair occupied by the sleeping Si, and kicked irritably at his foot.

"Hey!" he said. "A couple of you guys take this good-for-nothing stiff upstairs, and put him to bed. We'll have to play without a guitar tonight, damn him! Frankie, he's your roommate. Get going!"

Frankie arose sullenly, and tried to wake Si, but without success. Finally, with Jimmy's help, he managed to arouse the sleeping guitarist long enough to get him out of the room.

Andy looked after the departing trio, his eyes narrowed. Then he shouted: "And where in hell's Pete? He's supposed to be the handy man around here. What do I pay him for?"

"Pete's wife is having a baby," Max contributed in a soothing voice, "and I told him he could have the day off. He should have been back by now, but it's storming outside, and I guess the busses couldn't—"

"*You* told him!" Andy's face was suffused with rage, the mean lines about the mouth giving him an unprepossessing appearance. "I give the orders around here, you lousy fathead! Now who's going to handle those lights for me on my vocal solo?"

"Oh, pipe down!" Max said wearily. "I'll handle the lights for you tonight. The switch box is right on the bandstand, and there's nothing to it. If Pete can do it, I can."

"Well, see that you do it right!" Andy admonished. "Are you sure you know when the overhead lights go out, and the spot goes on?"

"Sure, sure," Max said, relieved at Andy's acceptance of the situation. "I'll come out just before the fourth number in this set. That's the *Headlined* song, right?" At Andy's nod of agreement, he continued: "O.K., then, I'll listen first to the nine o'clock news. That'll give me plenty of time. Oops!" Max looked at his wrist watch. "It's nine already." He waddled over to the combination radio and record player. Snapping on the radio, he settled down painfully into the armchair nearby. A smooth metallic voice broke in:

". . . And latest meteorological reports say that a low storm has settled over New York and New Jersey. The blizzard is furious, and will go down in history as one of our severest snow and ice storms. Several severe accidents have already been reported. The police department warns all motorists to stay off the roads. And now for the latest news bulletins. London: Prime Minister—"

But Andy had stalked out, and the rest of the band followed him silently out of the room and onto the bandstand.

# 4

As the musicians took their places, Jack noticed that the instruments were grouped informally. At the extreme left and a little in front of the others was Andy's stand, the one he used when he played the trombone with the band. Next to that were the two stands for the trumpeters, Buddy and Jimmy, close together. Then came a group of three stands for the saxophones, Ray, Tony, and Windy; a little apart was Jack's place for the bass fiddle. Frankie, with all the paraphernalia and equipment necessary to a drummer, was next; and at the extreme right was the concert Steinway with its wing up, looking very imposing. The fact that the bandstand spread practically the entire width of the dance hall permitted this straight-line arrangement.

A girl and boy had been sitting on the edge of the platform. When Andy appeared in the vanguard of the band, they jumped up with excitement and applauded violently. There was an eerie echo from the applause in the great, shadowy hall—eerie, and somehow a little mocking in its emptiness.

"Andy! Andy Parker!" cried the boy eagerly. "We've been waiting ages for you!"

The youngster was dressed in the style assumed by up-to-date "sharpies"; trousers almost up to the armpits, and pegged to about twelve inches at the duffs; loudly striped shirt; and over it, a bulky, clumsy-looking jacket that came almost to his knees. He was young, not more than eighteen.

Scrambling up the platform, scorning to use the steps, he shoved a menu under Andy's nose, and said; "Please autograph this for my girl, please?"

Andy smiled in high good humor as he complied with the request. To Jack, who was watching him, there seemed to be an amazing transformation in the man's personality. His face took on a suavity, and as he spoke, his voice had a pleasant ring. It was hard to believe that this amiable man with the I'm-here-to-please-you manner and the male shrew who quarreled so incessantly with his musicians were the same person. Jack had been wondering how such an obnoxious individual had managed to stay on top so long in a field where a pleasant personality was so all-important. Now, watching his charming behavior toward the youngsters, Jack understood. Andy wasn't so dumb!

"Sorry to have kept such a pretty young lady waiting," said Andy with a pleasant smile, eyeing the young lady up and down significantly.

"And we drove all the way from Brooklyn in this awful weather just to hear you sing," broke in the girl, flushing under Andy's experienced scrutiny. She swung her long legs in their striped ankle socks and stylishly dirty saddle oxfords. "Us and another couple. They're still eating in one of the booths. And I think there are two more couples from Flatbush waiting, too."

"Let me see now," drawled Andy. "What can I do to atone for that awful trip from Brooklyn? Just name it."

The girl clapped her hands in rhythm, chanting slowly:

"We want a CON-ga! We want a CON-ga!"

"Right-o, Sugar," said Andy, giving her a sultry look, while his voice dripped honey. "Next set, you get the conga. And I want to see you leading the conga line."

"Aren't enough people here, but I'll do my best." And the girl gave her companion an appraising look as she compared his awkward youth unfavorably with Andy's polished maturity. Windy had said that women couldn't resist him. Jack saw now what Windy meant.

"Come on, boys," said Andy, picking up his trombone. "Didn't you hear the young lady saying she wanted music? Let's get going with *Bye, Bye, Blues*. One two *three!*" And the band swung into the hot arrangement.

Jack felt a thrill of excitement rise within him as he began plucking away at his bull fiddle. It was his first experience with a really good band: all excellent players doing justice to inspired arrangements, all working together as smoothly as though dissension had never entered their minds. The brass came in true and sweet, with a broad, easy tone, and the drummer sent them smoothly into the rhythm. The guitarist was missing, of course, but the remainder of the rhythm section didn't permit the lack to become apparent. Andy's hot licks as he swung on the trombone were enough to send Jack up to seventh heaven. What a musician! You could forgive a player like that almost anything.

Jack had been keeping his eyes on his music, but by the time Buddy had swung into his second chorus trumpet solo, he had recovered from his temporary nervousness enough to take occasional swift glances at the dance floor. The immense, shadowy hall was practically deserted, and contained just a few young dancers lindy-hopping to the fast music. All were dressed like the young couple who had spoken previously to Andy: the boys in peg-pants, and the girls in sweaters, skirts, and anklets. All but one girl, rather short in height, who was dressed in an elaborate evening gown which was much too sophisticated for her blonde youthfulness. She was dancing conservatively with a youth not much taller than herself.

Her formal gown made an incongruous appearance in the rustic surroundings of the Casino, and Jack wondered idly who she could be. Probably one of the flightier residents of Brooklyn, he decided, then went back to his music, plucking strenuously away at his instrument, as the arrangement headed into the very hot and very loud climax. A trumpet, Buddy's, slid up to a high note, held it while the band jammed away under it, then, with a thump of the bass drum, the song was over.

Jack was exhilarated. What a band! And he was part of it! Then he remembered with a throb of pleasure that Lee was to do the vocal on the next number, *Stormy Weather*. He waited for the lights to dim, but when Andy started them off immediately, Jack realized with a stab of resentment that Andy wouldn't permit a spotlight on Lee. He wanted all the limelight for himself. And the arrangement wasn't a vocal arrangement at all, in which a singer is featured. It was a dance arrangement, in which the vocalist only came in on the second chorus. Andy, as Jack expected now, came right in at the beginning with a trombone solo for the first chorus. But—he certainly was good!

Andy's trombone wailed into the blue notes of *Stormy Weather* like a soul in torment. He had complete mastery over his instrument, and the tone was true and full, with all the nuances of which a trombone is capable. Pure "schmaltz."

The melody finally throbbed to its close, and suddenly Lee was at the microphone in the center of the bandstand, singing into the tiny, glittery ball which carried her low, sweet voice miraculously to every corner of the great low-ceilinged room. Jack's mind was hardly on his work, as he watched her standing there, straight and slim. Her black hair, with a flashing ornament catching a cluster of curls on top, swayed on her smooth bare shoulders as she turned her head, singing to all corners of the room.

The dancers had stopped to listen, and they came closer to the platform. Jack felt proud of her—proud, and somehow resentful of the fact that she was singing to just a handful of kids with a boss like Andy. She should be singing into a mike at NBC, or CBS, her lovely voice carried into millions of homes. She'd never get the recognition she deserved singing for Andy Parker. He didn't give her a chance.

Jack watched the white shoulders, the long, slim hands held out gracefully as if in appeal:

"Keeps raining all the ti-ime . . ."

Her voice was husky with the sorrow of disappointed lovers all the world over. Jack's thought veered as he played mechanically, unable to keep his eyes off her. Maybe she did care for someone. A girl like that could have her choice of anyone, so what could she ever see in a guy like him? What an unutterable fool he was! What made him think he could even think of her that way? What could he offer her? He tried to put those depressing thoughts from him, but his fancies ran on. She was the moon, and he was a stupid child crying for it; she was a goddess and he was a mortal; she was fame and success, and he—he was just plenty of nothing! "Say," a little voice in his mind taunted him, "you certainly got bitten bad, didn't you? Don't you know better?" Oh, hell! What a lamebrain he was to let a synthetic Tin Pan Alley product affect him that way.

Lee was through, and as she walked slowly to the right of the bandstand, Andy took over again for the remaining half chorus, and then the band brought the song to a close on a throbbing blues chord.

The musicians changed their music. He'd have to keep his mind on this one, *Booglie-Wooglie Piggie*. This was where the boys came in on the chorus, singing in unison.

The drummer started off with an insidious, cajoling rhythm—eight to the bar—that indescribable, nerve-tingling beat that sets the heart to dancing. Primitive?

Barbaric? Uncivilized? Well, perhaps, but at least it was vital and fresh and alive. There was nothing decadent about that boogie-woogie rhythm. All serious music started with the people; all good composers went directly to the folk sources for a good part of their material. Some day someone would do for boogie-woogie what Gershwin did for early jazz. But it would take another genius—a genius with humble beginnings, someone who had sweated over that beat in a band. Jack's thoughts suddenly stopped wandering, and gave attention to what his ears were hearing.

The piano had come in with a powerful, rhythmic figure in the bass, and now it had the first chorus to itself as solo, accompanied only by the rhythm section. And what a piano! Iggy's strong left hand beat out the rhythm, while his right hand played variations on the original tune that were nothing short of inspired. It seemed almost impossible for only two hands to be getting all that music out of one instrument. That repeated bass had an almost hypnotic effect. Iggy had something rare—originality combined with technique, and a beat that defied description; a beat that never in this world could be adequately transcribed to paper. Iggy loved what he was doing; that was obvious. But he loved it with understanding, and a knowledge of its limitations, as well as a realization of its possibilities which he explored to the full. His improvisation came to an end with a brilliant crescendo, and the rest of the band took over.

The band came in as an anti-climax, as far as Jack was concerned. Any amateur would have known that boogie-woogie was piano music, not suited to an orchestra at all. Piano music only—four hand piano music preferably, as in the wonderful Negro team of Ammons and Lewis—but by all means a piano was necessary, with someone like that moody young Iggy to play it. Probably that boy would be able to compose if he wanted to badly enough. He should, if he could improvise that way. After all, improvisation was composing right at the instrument.

Jack had forgotten his good intentions of keeping his mind solely on playing and reading the music before him, and he chanted mechanically with the rest of the band:

"Oink-oink; Boog-ul-lie woog-ul-lie" in the places indicated on his manuscript. He might just as well have been listening to Iggy's solo again, and he went over it in his mind with admiration and envy. If he only had a gift like that! Genius and good looks—what a combination! Yet here he was, playing second fiddle to a rat like Andy!

Then Jack listened again with delight, for the canny arranger had given the closing bars back into Iggy's capable hands, and he did the score justice. Jack sighed in something that was very close to ecstasy as the piano tinkled to a muted close, all the more exciting for being so subdued. Then, a rapid da-da-da-DUM! and it was over.

There was a violent burst of applause that was surprising in its volume, coming as it did from such a small audience. A shrill young enthusiast called out:

"Yay, Iggy! We want more! Hurry and make with that piano!"

Iggy stood up, his dark, weary eyes lighting up as he smiled shyly. He bowed in recognition of the applause. Then Jack noticed that a shadow crossed Andy's face as he stood in his place at the end of the platform. It was rage, rage and jealousy at this adoration the small though appreciative audience felt for the pianist. Andy was about to rap on his stand for the band to begin the next number, but he stopped when he noticed the girl in the formal gown leaving her escort in the middle of the floor, and coming over to the bandstand.

"Andy," she called plaintively, "when are you going to play our song?" Her rosebud lips, which were normally half open (probably a habit acquired as a result of an adenoidal childhood), were pouting, and the round cheeks and blue child's eyes looked completely out of harmony with the revealing, backless gown made of alternate panels of cerise and chartreuse chiffon. A wide jeweled belt was fastened so tightly about her waist that her soft plump figure resembled a full grain sack tied tightly in the middle. The unfortunate resemblance was heightened by the fact that she was very short, certainly not over five feet tall. She gave her corn-colored, heavily lacquered page boy bob a petulant toss, and said with a coaxing air:

"Come on, Andy, dear. Please—play it for Kitty. Play *Headlined in My Heart,* pretty please?"

Kitty! So this was Max's daughter! Jack examined her with curiosity. He could see, now that he looked for it, the resemblance between the girl and her father. Kitty, the girl that Andy was playing around with in Andy's own peculiar way. Why, she was young enough to be his daughter! No wonder Max was so worried. This child obviously didn't know what it was all about, poor kid . . .

Andy looked down at her with some annoyance. It was clear that he resented her implied ownership of him. But he conquered his irritation with an effort, and answered pleasantly enough in a low voice: "So help me, my sweet, I was just going to play it. It's next on our schedule."

"Will you sing it to *me*, Andy; please?" And she smiled an enchanting little-girl smile.

"Psssst!" Jack turned to his right, and saw Windy shaking his head, an expression of loathing on his chubby face. "That dopey dame is screwy about him!" he whispered.

Jack put his forefinger to his throat, and made a slitting motion in reply. Windy smiled, and whispered: "Don't you do it. He isn't worth it."

Then Jack noticed with a start that Max was standing against the wall to his right, watching his daughter flirting with Andy. The expression on Max's face was bitter—horribly and murderously bitter. "God," thought Jack, "I wouldn't care to have anyone feel that way about me! Not that I can blame him. She's so young. . . ."

Kitty finally went back to her partner, and as Max pressed a switch, the light over the bandstand started dimming. Then the platform was in complete darkness, and small lights on the inside of the music stands went on, throwing their tiny beams of light directly on the sheets of music. A large electrical contraption on the ceiling over the dance floor lit up, and started slowly revolving. As it revolved, small colored blobs of light slithered in one direction around the room. It was dark now, and a little weird.

Then a bright spotlight flashed directly on the mike, and there stood Andy, bathed in its golden light. Nothing else in the hall was now visible, nothing but Andy. He lifted his hand, brought it down sharply, and the band started playing in a slow, syncopated blues rhythm.

Jack was thoroughly familiar with this arrangement, having listened to the record countless times. The saxes and rhythm played a soft four-bar introduction, and Andy started singing on the upbeat of the next bar, his voice soaring up, then down, following the odd modulation of the song:

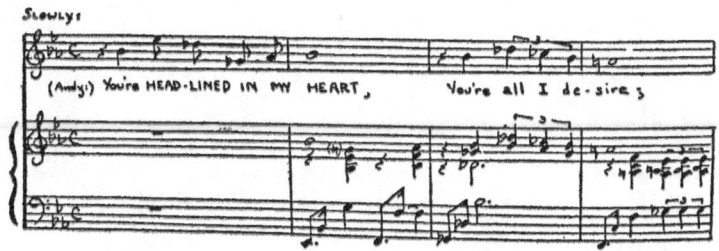

It was a simple melody—simple, yet at the same time, strange. And Andy's voice was perfect for a mike, the kind that has few overtones to lose in the process of amplification. He knew the art of singing to an audience, too, all the tricks were part of his technique. He turned, facing first one way, then the other, but his lips were never far from the gleaming ball before him. . . .

You're HEAD-LINED IN MY HEART . . .    in let-ters of Fire;

The orchestra, invisible behind him, came in on the pause, subdued, yet full. Jack watched Andy's back, seeing him standing there in the center of the spotlight. He had to admit, although reluctantly, that in spite of his slim build, Andy's appearance left nothing to be desired. The wavy, honey-colored hair borrowed golden gleams from the strong light above him, and his shoulders, amazingly powerful (or was that just excellent tailoring?), set off the thin waist and narrow hips. Although Jack couldn't see his face, he could picture how Andy would look as he sang those lyrics: yearning and romantic, so that every female in the hall would be certain that he was singing to her, and her alone. But then, wasn't that essentially the reason for the spectacular success of all crooners? That intimate, we're-all-alone manner— Well, Andy was all alone there on the platform, all alone in the light. No one else was visible. All was dark, and suddenly, the darkness took on a smothering quality . . .

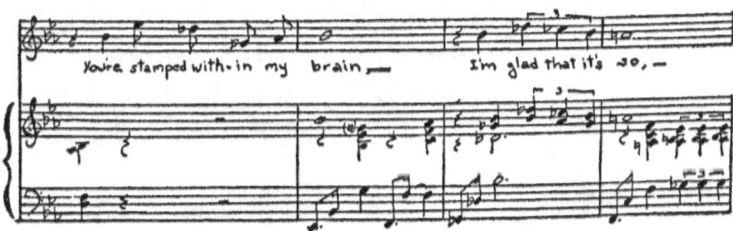

Jack's mind turned to Lee with an accompanying flutter of the heart. She certainly seemed to be immune to Andy's powerful magnetism. They hadn't even spoken to each other civilly, and what exchange there had been was filled with an open animosity. From Andy's attitude, it was apparent that he had tried to ingratiate himself with her, but hadn't gotten to first base. So Andy was out. But what about the pianist? Lee had said he was carrying the torch for someone else, but she hadn't mentioned what her feelings toward him were . . .

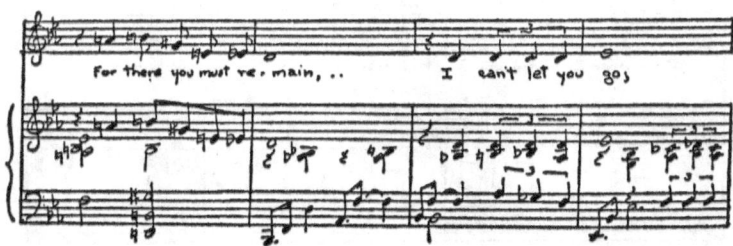

"You'll have to let her go," Jack thought in despair, the mood of the song catching him in its net, as songs have a way of doing. "Let her go?" he mocked himself. "Why, you never had her, so how could you let her go?" Still, she had seemed to like him a little in that brief interchange outside the door—or was that only her natural politeness?

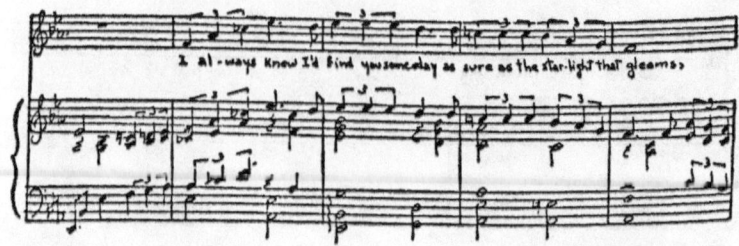

Andy's voice was a counter melody to the sweet pain in his heart. So he had found her. So what? It would be better to forget her—think of something else—anything else. Poor Rosanne Abbott, for instance, who had committed suicide for no apparent reason, when she had everything to live for. Little, infatuated Kitty, who was making a fool of herself over a rat like Andy. Max, who had to watch his daughter letting herself in for so much unhappiness . . .

Andy was moving into the few bars ending the release . . .

Jack suddenly felt worn and tired. That darkness, with the small masses of light moving so noiselessly, so uncannily . . . He began to feel apprehensive. A cold lump of foreboding had lodged itself in the pit of his stomach with an almost physical intensity, and he couldn't rid himself of it. This empty, gloomy place had gotten on his nerves. "Stop acting like an old maid afraid of her shadow," he jeered at himself. "You're just tireder than you realized, what with that long and difficult trip. And you're disappointed because you're not playing to a full house. And you didn't expect the boys to fight around as they did with Andy. You had expected fun and comradeship . . . But it's about time you stopped living in a fairy tale. You're a big boy now." But the mood stayed. He couldn't exorcise it. "All right, then," he commanded himself, "listen to that marvelous arrangement. That's still good, isn't it? Well— isn't it? . . ."

Hell! Even that fell flat. The wire brushes of the drummer slithered softly in the slow beat of the rhythm, accompanying the low, full chords of the piano. The muted trumpets sounded dreamily, as from a distance, moving down in harmony in sustained half notes against the soaring triplets of the saxophone obbligato. All this against the whole note that Andy held. There it was, his favorite measure, and because of this crazy mood that possessed him, even that sounded empty—empty, and futile, and meaningless . . .

Andy took a breath. . . .

And ... no....

The whole world exploded right in Jack's ear! His head buzzed. The hall was filled with sound and echoes of sound reverberating. A girl's scream tore through the darkness. He couldn't move, and his hand holding the bull fiddle seemed to be glued there. The explosion had bewitched him into immobility.

Andy, in front of the microphone, was standing rigid—
rigid, and horribly still. A word gargled unreleased in this
throat. What was wrong? Why didn't Andy continue?

Then, slowly, vaguely, like the motion of a mass seen
under water, Andy wavered. He slid against the chromium
stem, crumpling like a smashed marionette. And with a
sickening thud, the bandleader and the microphone top-
pled over the edge of the platform together, onto the floor
below.

# 5

The music died away in jagged moans. For a moment there was silence. Then, suddenly, breathless little sounds of confusion made themselves heard. Chairs were scraped out of the way, music sheets rustled to the floor as the musicians got up hastily, brass instruments clanged against the metal music racks; but through it all, no one spoke. There seemed to be a conspiracy of silence, of wordlessness, as though they had all been stricken dumb. And all the time the darkness closed in on them oppressively, closed in and pushed them toward that center of catastrophe—that crumpled form that was Andy Parker, lying in the semicircle of light against the bandstand. Then someone found his voice, and harsh male tones commanded: "The lights! Hurry! Put those lights on!" The piercing shriek of a woman resounded again; and the lights suddenly glared on.

Kitty was there at Andy's side, kneeling down, and tugging at his inert body.

"Andy! Andy, darling! Speak to me, please. It's Kitty. Don't you hear me? Andy!" Her voice was a crescendo of grief and fear.

She tried vainly to turn his body over, and then looked down at her hands with a horror-stricken expression. They were sticky, and wet, and red. . . . And down the front of her gay gown were long splashes of the same thick red, contrasting horribly with the cerise and chartreuse . . .

"It's blood!" she whispered, her eyes wide with terror. "Blood—Andy's blood! He's dead—*dead*—DEAD!" And as the dreadful realization penetrated her mind, scream after scream tore hysterically from her throat.

"Kitty! Kitty! Stop it!" Max was at her side, trying to pull her away from Andy. He shook her violently as her screams continued. "Stop it, I say! I told you not to come to the Casino tonight. Why did you disobey me, you foolish child?" His voice was terrible to hear, and once more Jack felt the chill of foreboding creep up his spine.

Kitty stopped her screaming, and wrenched away from her father.

"Get away from me!" she shrieked. "Keep your hands off me! You're glad he's dead—I know you are! You hated him!" And she began to sob, great racking sobs.

"Kitty!" Max's face turned a gray-white. "You don't know what you are saying!"

The sounds of confusion now made themselves heard above the tense moment. The musicians and dancers gathered around the still form on the floor, jostling and pushing their way to get a better look. Servants and waiters and bus boys came rushing in from the kitchen, craning their necks, and asking questions in soft, horrified whispers. With fascinated eyes, they watched a dark, wet stain spreading slowly over the blue of Andy's evening jacket.

Then a young voice said hesitantly: "Get a doctor, maybe he's still alive!" And almost simultaneously, a girl shouted hysterically:

"Stand back! Give him air!"

And Buddy's voice answered back in a clear, mocking whisper: "Air? Air won't do *him* any good now!—He needs to be vulcanized!"

Again there were confused murmurs. Everyone was at a loss. Someone suggested phoning for a doctor anyway, and was informed that the phone wasn't working.

And then the boy who had been dancing with Kitty detached himself from the group, saying: "I'm a medical student at the 'U.' Maybe I can help." No one answered, so he knelt down beside the inert figure. Everyone's eyes were fastened on him as he lifted the limp wrist and felt the pulse with a professional air.

"No pulse at all," the boy volunteered solemnly. He turned Andy face up with some difficulty, since no one seemed disposed to help him. Feeling for the heart, he shook his head, and turned the body face down again. The blood gushed forth suddenly, and the youngster turned pale. He looked unwillingly at the wound on the back, and touched it gingerly with fingers that trembled. He cleared his throat, then looked up at those surrounding him, and announced in a shaking voice:

"He's dead, no doubt about it! Killed instantly." He eyed the stain again dubiously. "I—I think he was shot through the heart . . ."

"The heart—or a reasonable facsimile thereof . . ."

"Buddy!" Ray's voice, echoing loudly, was knife-sharp. "This is hardly the place nor the time for your mistaken sense of humor. He's dead!"

"You're—you're sure he's dead, Butch?" Max's voice quavered uncertainly.

"Yep!" the boy answered. "I guess he was killed instantly. He must have been. Damn," he muttered to himself, "why did I have to cut so many of my anatomy classes!" He turned the body over again, looking puzzled. The white expanse of shirt front was clean and unstained. "Let's see, now. The bullet must still be inside . . ." The full implications of what he was saying suddenly occurred to him as well as to the whole group.

"Why—why—" His face turned white, and his eyes dilated. "A bullet! That means *murder!*"

Murder! The word fell like a rock into the thick silence. A wave of dread, almost tangible, splashed in ever widening circles, and broke into the consciousness of the people standing about.

"No, no!" Kitty wailed, trying to tear herself from her father's arms. "He isn't dead! He can't be! Tell them you're not, Andy. We're engaged . . . Tell them!" She struggled, but her father held her fast, a look of anguish on his round, creased face.

The young dancers had gathered in a little knot. They tried hard to look solemn, but their excitement broke through. They found a weird pleasure in this scene, pleasure that they were in on something that promised to be the biggest thing in their lives. "They don't really believe it," thought Jack as he watched them trying to suppress their obvious enjoyment. "They think it's something staged for their benefit, like a play—just something to amuse them. And, come to think of it, do I believe it? No—it didn't really happen. It couldn't! Things like this don't happen in real life. They simply don't. They happen to unknowns in newspapers—an unidentified man found dead on the corner of such-and-such a street; they happen to characters in pulp magazines—to anyone but us."

Ray broke into Jack's thoughts, his voice loud in the oppressive silence that the medical student's announcement had created. Ray was still holding his saxophone in his hand, its supporting cord around his neck.

"You shouldn't have touched anything, you know," he stated solemnly, his eyes accusing behind the heavy spectacles. "Not till the police get here. This is more serious than any of you seem to realize." He hesitated, then boldly uttered the thought that was uppermost in everyone's mind. "Someone here is a criminal—a murderer. Someone here killed him!"

"Oh stop declaiming," said Buddy, moving restlessly, and shifting his trumpet to the other hand. "We're not morons. Andy obviously didn't commit suicide."

Lee appeared on the bandstand, stepping out from between the curtains. "What happened? Why isn't the band playing . . . ?" Then the scene in front of her penetrated. The circle of people around the ominously crumpled figure—the red puddle spreading on the floor—

She ran down the platform steps, her eyes wide, and a look of fear distorting her face. She pushed through the group, and looked down.

"Why, it's—it's Andy—" Her voice trailed off interrogatively.

"You mean it *was* Andy," said Frankie, scratching nervously at his cheek.

"He's dead, Lee," said Ray. "Murdered! That's a bullet wound in his back."

"And on him it looks good!" Buddy flung out defiantly.

"Oh, no!" Lee cried out. "Andy can't be— Who—?"

Ray shrugged his shoulders, looking at the body with a curious detachment.

Jack moved toward Lee with a protective movement, but Iggy was there first, taking her arm, steadying her, and talking to her in a soothing voice. "Easy, there, Lee. There's nothing anyone can do about it now. Steady."

The sounds of Kitty's sobs penetrated Lee's fascinated preoccupation with the still figure on the floor. She gave a sharp exclamation of pity, and moved toward the girl with outstretched arms.

"Kitty, dear, don't take it so hard. He wasn't worth it."

Kitty shrank from her. "Don't touch me," she cried. "Don't touch me! You hated him, too. Everyone here hated

him! Everyone but me—and I loved him! I'll always love
him. I'll never forget him!" And the tears, black with mas-
cara, streaked down her cheeks unchecked. She looked
pathetically like a little girl masquerading in a grown-up's
make-up. Max had been holding her back, but now she
tore from his grasp and ran to the young medical student.

"Butch!" She clutched nervously at his arm. "Butch,
tell them he isn't dead!" He took out his handkerchief, and
tried awkwardly to dry her tears;

"Don't, Kitty," he said, his voice tender. "Don't take it
that way."

She held on to his arm like a drowning man grasping at
a straw. "It's all a dream, isn't it, Butch? Just a bad dream.
Make me wake up, please. Oh, Andy!" And she buried her
head in his shoulder. He looked not at all displeased for a
moment; then, taking a hasty glance at the body, he shook
his head helplessly. It did seem uncommonly like a nightmare to him, too.

Max observed her in Butch's arms, and despite the fact
that she had turned from him, he had a strangely satisfied
look on his face—satisfied and triumphant and at peace
with himself.

Everyone still stood around aimlessly, making aimless
remarks, giving unnecessary advice. Suddenly, Jack could
contain himself no longer.

"I'm going for the police," he announced, "storm or no
storm. After all, this is murder, and—"

"But you can't go now," Max interrupted quickly. "You
heard what the radio announcer said. It's suicide to travel
in this weather, especially on that dirt road to get to the
state highway. You'll never make it."

"He's right, Jack," said Windy, now beside Jack. "You'll
never get to a cop now, and where would you find a phone
that's working?"

"We'll have to wait till the company repairs the phones at the break," agreed Ray. "It won't be long, I suppose."

"I guess you're right," Jack admitted reluctantly. "Only—well, I hate this inaction. There must be something we can do."

"Why don't you take charge, Jack?" suggested Windy. "Maybe you can clean this mess up before the police get here."

"Me?" asked Jack incredulously. "What do I know about it?"

"Yeah!" said Frankie, knocking his drum sticks against his thigh. "Who is he to take charge?"

"Well, you boys couldn't know about it," announced Windy, "but it happens that Jack had a job as a detective for a while. He quit that job to come here tonight, as a matter of fact."

"You mean—on the police force?" asked Iggy, looking suspiciously at Jack's long, lean height.

"Oh, no!" Jack denied hastily, wondering whether to let them in on the fact that he had had exactly two weeks experience at doing nothing even remotely connected with detection. "I was with a private agency."

"I guess that puts you in a position of knowing more than we do about those things," said Iggy.

"But—" Jack started protesting.

"It's up to you to tell us what to do now," said Windy, flashing him a warning glance.

Jack scratched his red head in dismay. How should he know what to do? This certainly was a fine fix Windy had put him in. He cursed silently at the conversational impulse that had led him to tell Windy about his peculiar and fragmentary experience as a private detective. Then suddenly an adventurous feeling took possession of him. What harm could he possibly do by attempting some sort of investigation? He'd have to assume the responsibility, but it would be fun to play at being a real detective. Besides, the choice seemed to be out of his hands. They had accepted, although rather indifferently, the fact that he was in temporary charge.

Jimmy, the second trumpeter, spoke up, addressing Jack as the nominal head of the group. "Gosh, it's too bad we don't broadcast tonight," he said, his face eager and alive, his features still blurred with the softness of youth. "'Cause if we did, the broadcasting company would connect us onto the network about eleven o'clock, and we could send an SOS by radio. Boy, what a sensation that would make!"

"Well, we are not broadcasting for a couple of days, so there's no use thinking about it," said Ray, the logical.

"I don't know about the rest of you guys," Frankie broke in nervously, "but I could sure stand a drink!"

The youngsters, who had remained close to each other as if for protection, shifted restlessly.

"Hey! What happens to us?" asked one of the more obviously "sharpie" of the lot. "If the roads are that bad, how do we get home?"

"I knew we shouldn't have come in this awful weather," said a girl with a huge bow on her brown curls, a worried expression on her face. "My mother'll go daffy worrying about me if I don't get home tonight."

"Yes, and they say the phones are out of order," chimed in another girl gloomily, "so we can't even let our folks know what's happened. No matter what else they say about it, things like this don't happen in Brooklyn."

The youngsters all looked troubled now. Before, it had just been a lark, but now they were caught too.

"There's only one thing you kids can do," said Max, coming forward. "You'll have to stay overnight. I have plenty of room in the hotel, if the girls are willing to sleep two girls in a room. It's happened before that some guests of the Casino were stranded here in bad weather, only that time the phones were O.K. Believe me," he concurred heartily, "I wish I was in Brooklyn too, now!"

"But what'll my mother say?" the first girl asked anxiously.

"Don't be silly," another girl reprimanded her with a practical air. "When she hears about it she'll be glad that you were able to stay over some place safe. Even if she does worry about it tonight, it won't matter so much as long as we turn up safe tomorrow."

"Golly!" one of the boys broke out in excitement. "Betcha we get our pictures in the papers. Imagine—being here when Andy Parker was murdered! It's just like a movie!" His eyes popped as he looked again at the figure on the floor.

Jack decided that it was about time he took charge. "Max, you take these kids wherever it is you're going to put them," he ordered. "And after that, we'll have to do something about—about Andy. We can't just leave him lying there like that, even if the police don't like it."

"That's true," concurred Ray. "He can't stay there all night."

"Take him up to his room," suggested Max.

"No," objected Ray. "That's my room, too. I share a room with him, you know."

"What's the difference?" asked Max impatiently. "You can take another room. There are some spares upstairs."

"O.K.," said Jack. "Let's go." But as they bent down to pick up the body, Kitty started screaming again.

"Look, Mr. Harris," suggested Butch as he held her helplessly, "I think you'd better take Kitty to her room in the hotel."

"I'll go with her, too," offered Lee. "And I'll stay with her tonight. She's too hysterical to stay alone. She needs a glass of hot milk and an aspirin."

Kitty made no protest, and Max sighed with relief. His eye fell on the kitchen staff still conversing in awed whispers, and he ordered them peremptorily back to their posts. Then he and Lee supporting Kitty, with Butch trailing ineffectively in their wake, vanished into the exit leading to the kitchen and the hotel. The servants followed, looking back over their shoulders at the grim scene they were leaving behind them.

"Come on, you kids," ordered Jack. "Go along with them. Max will show you to your rooms." The boys looked mutinous, but seeing the unfriendly faces of the other musicians, some of who backed up Jack's orders with muttered exclamations of "Scram!" and "Go on, beat it!" they left hastily after the others.

When they had gone, Jack, who had discovered his bow still clutched tightly in his hand, replaced it near his instrument on the platform, and turned again to the task of getting Andy upstairs. Buddy and Ray helped him. All together, they managed to carry him down the length of the dance floor, to the stairway, and up the stairs. It was surprising how heavy Andy was. Only it really wasn't Andy any longer. It was nothing now, just a mass of dead matter. Jack felt rather than saw the gruesome trail of thick red that trickled along their path.

"In here," said Ray, stopping before a door. Iggy and Windy, who had followed along in case help should be needed, ran ahead to the door, and Iggy flung it open quickly.

They deposited the body on the nearest bed, and covered it with the sheet.

"Well, what do we do now?" asked Buddy. "Say a prayer?"

The others ignored him, but he continued cynically: "We could at least say a poem, or something. How about *To a Louse,* by Robert Burns?"

"Buddy!" remonstrated Ray, with asperity. "You seem to think this is a huge joke. It's not funny, and further-more, it's in damned bad taste."

Jack had been looking about him, examining the room with interest. It was exactly like his and Windy's. He went to the bathroom door, tried the knob, and opened it. He saw nothing of any value in the small though adequately equipped bathroom, and returned.

"Who has the other room opening out from the bath-room?" he asked.

"It's empty," answered Ray, looking at him curiously. "Why?"

"Nothing. I just wondered."

"I suppose I'll have to take it tonight," said Ray. "Can't share a room with Andy tonight," he continued with a shrug, lighting a cigarette, "I'll take my things out later, though. I think I'll have a drink first, as Frankie suggested."

"Frankie probably corralled the whole supply from the bar by now," said Buddy, his eyes fastened on the sheeted figure on the bed. "If you want any, you'd better go down quick. He and Si—they're half human, half sponge."

Iggy suddenly pointed to Jack's suit in dismay. "Your jacket is—dirty," he said, looking sick. He had a red splash on his own shirt front.

"We'll all have to change," said Jack with a squeamish look at himself and the others. "This—this blood—" They certainly looked gory.

"Don't you think," asked Ray, "that we'd better see whether Si is still in his room?"

"What are you driving at, Ray?" asked Iggy, the cigarette he had been trying to light quivering in his long, sensitive fin-gers. "You don't think that something's happened to Si, too?"

"No, I don't think anything has happened to Si, but—" Ray's voice took on significant overtones—"perhaps he's the one who—" His voice trailed away, full of meaning.

They looked at each other, and Jack forgot about his bloody clothes. "What are we waiting for, then?" he cried. "Let's go to his room, and see if he really is sleeping his drunk off." He dashed out of the room, asking: "Which is his room?"

The others followed him. "Here," said Ray, pausing outside one of the bedroom doors in the corridor. "He and Frank are roommates."

"Well, open it!" Jack commanded impatiently, as Ray listened cautiously against the door.

"Oh, yes?" Ray exclaimed, keeping his voice low. "You forget that the person who killed Andy has a gun!"

"What are you afraid of?" asked Jack scornfully. "I saw Jimmy and Frankie help Si out of the lounge, and he certainly was tight." He turned the knob and, opening the door, entered the room, the others close behind him.

Si was lying on the bedspread, his legs sprawling, and his hands outflung in the complete abandon of sleep. His fair, broad-boned face was flushed, his mouth loosely open, and his breathing was heavy and raucous.

Jack bent over the bed and shook him violently. "Hey, Si," he shouted. "Si! Get up, do you hear? Wake up!"

Si opened his eyes and looked stupidly at Jack. "Go 'way," he said thickly. "Go 'way! I don't know you." And he turned on his side, and started his heavy regular breathing once again.

"He's not faking, if that's what you meant, Ray," said Jack. "He's really dead drunk. There's hardly any possibility that he could have done it while he was drunk, but if he did, the gun ought to be somewhere around here."

He turned to the bureau near Si's bed, opened the drawers, and began examining their contents.

"Hey!" Buddy objected. "Si won't like that, and neither will Frankie."

"Andy didn't like it either," said Jack, searching busily.

"Jack's right," said Windy. "I'm going to help." And he got to work. They went over the room carefully, searching under the mattresses, in the bureau drawers, and in every possible hiding place. But to no avail. No gun was to be found. And Si slept on undisturbed.

"Well, Ray," Jack said presently, "it looks as if you were wrong about Si. There's no gun in this room. We'll have to look for it elsewhere."

"I'm going to change," said Iggy, crushing his cigarette stub underfoot.

"Me, too," said Jack.

"I'll come with you, Jack, and wait," offered Windy.

"C'mon, Ray; I'll help you take your things into the next room so you can change there." And Buddy started for Andy's room.

"Buddy thinks I'm afraid to stay in that room alone with Andy," Ray said to the others, smiling an odd smile. "It's thoughtful of him to offer—thoughtful but unnecessary. Andy is dead. He can't hurt anyone now—not any more."

# 6

"Well, Windy," asked Jack, "what do you think of this business?" Windy was sitting on the bed, while Jack changed his tux for the suit he had driven up in.

"I don't know," Windy answered slowly. "It looks like someone didn't like Andy, to say the least."

"You're a fine one, you are!" Jack accused him. "Mixing me up in it! Why did you have to tell them I had a job as a detective? You know what a farce that job was."

"You're smart," announced Windy confidently. "Just as smart as those detectives on the police force. It shouldn't be any trouble for you to solve it. Besides, I don't see that there's much to solve."

"What do you mean?" asked Jack as he was adjusting his tie, so that the words emerged with a strangled sound.

"Honestly, now, who do you think could have done it? And who *would* have done it?"

"Well—" Jack hesitated.

"Exactly!" Windy exclaimed emphatically. "Max! You aren't blind. You saw how he looked every time he mentioned Andy. And did you see his face when Andy was speaking to his kid? Not that you can blame him, when you come right down to it."

"I don't think he did it," Jack said stubbornly.

"You mean you don't want to think so, but you really do, don't you?"

Jack continued fixing his tie in obstinate silence.

"Oh, what's the use of kidding ourselves?" said Windy after a moment's pause. "What reason have you to think he's innocent? And anyway, you don't have to do anything definite about it, you know. The police 'll take care of that. You can just sort of take charge to prevent panic. If the police do decide it was Max, maybe they won't get enough evidence to convict him."

"I don't care what you say," Jack insisted earnestly. "It—it just isn't logical, Windy. If he had wanted to kill him, why should he pick that time, when everyone was around? It's not like him."

"How do you know what's like him?" Windy asked seriously. "After all, what do you know about anyone? Sometimes you yourself never know what you're capable of. And besides, you've only just met Max. Understand, I'm not saying positively that he did it—only that he's the most likely person."

"Maybe you are right about him," Jack agreed reluctantly, "but there are some things I'd like to clear up."

"Now I'm sorry I shoved you into it," said Windy with a remorseful look on his round face. "I did it more for a joke than anything else. And now you're determined to mix yourself up in a mess that's none of your business or mine. We ought to let them fight it out by themselves."

"I'm in it now, Windy, and it's too late to do anything about it. Besides, I kind of like the idea. It's—it's—what's that word?—it intrigues me. And anyhow, I can't just back out now, after you told the fellows that I was a detective. It'll make me look like a damn fool."

"It's not the fellows you mind so much," Windy remarked shrewdly. "You're worried about the impression you'll make on the girl, Lee."

Jack picked up the bloody shirt he had taken off, and answered slowly: "You're a wise old owl, Windy. And maybe you're right about me being a show-off. But there's also this: A man was killed. He wasn't much good, I'll grant you that, and it doesn't look as though many people will be sorry to see him dead. Still, no one person has the right to take things into his own hands. We have laws for that. That's what our civilization is based on. And, incidentally, forget about Lee, eh?" The color mounted to his face, and the freckles stood out orange against the pink.

"O.K., Jack," said Windy with a pacifying air. "Don't get sore now. I didn't mean anything. Only I think I wished a big job onto you. For instance, you have to know things about whatchamacall'ems—about guns—you know."

"Ballistics?" supplied Jack.

"Yeah, that's what I mean, ballistics. And fingerprints. Do you think you can tackle it?"

Jack rubbed his red thatch until it stood on end. "The way you put it, Windy, it does sound like something too big for me to handle, but I can't lose anything by trying. And more important than the mechanical angle—the ballistics and fingerprints that you just mentioned—is the personal equation."

"What's that?" asked Windy with a blank look.

"I mean what these people are like, what their personalities are, and which ones hated Andy enough to kill him."

"Oh, you mean motives," said Windy helpfully.

"Yes, motives," agreed Jack, seizing on the word. "I was just reading an article on crime last week, and do you know the three most important reasons for murder?"

"O.K. I'll make like a stooge for you," laughed Windy. "What, Mr. Bones, are the three most important reasons for murder?"

"Money, love, and revenge, in that order. Every motive can be traced to one of those motives or a combination of them."

"So all you have to do," answered Windy to that, "is to find out who owed Andy money, who loved him, and who hated him, and you have the killer—a whole bandful, eh?"

"Oh, all right," Jack said irritably. "You needn't laugh at me. What can I lose by trying?"

"I don't mean to discourage you, Jack," said Windy. "I got you into it, and I'll do my best to help you out. So remember, you can count on me. I guess a guy like you is smart enough to do whatever you set out to do."

"Thanks, Windy. I guess we'd better go down and start Sherlocking, eh, Watson?"

"Just one thing more, Jack," said Windy, pausing at the door. "But please don't get mad, now, because I'm saying this just for your benefit. You seem to have tumbled hard for that singing gal. Women are the craziest people. You can't tell about them. So please be careful, won't you? You're a nice guy, and I hope you take my advice, so—"

"O.K., O.K., my friend," said Jack, grinning at Windy's earnest gravity. "Don't worry about me. I know the facts of life, and I'll be careful of the vampires."

As they walked down the long length of the hall to the bandstand, Jack remembered that he had walked that path to the lounge for the first time just a short time before—but with such a difference! Now there was a colored porter on his knees, a pan of soapy water beside him, scrubbing gingerly at the stains that had been Andy's life blood.

The porter looked apprehensively behind him when he heard their footsteps echoing in the dance hall, then sighed with relief when he saw the musicians. He arose from the floor and stretched painfully, while the cloth in his hand dripped pinkly.

"Those stains sure are stubborn!" he announced, his teeth gleaming a startled white in his ebony face. He lowered his voice to a hissing whisper, and his eyes rolled uneasily. "Blood is always hahd to git rid of—in more ways than one! Such doin's, mah goodness! 'Nuff excitement to last me a while!"

Jack smiled at him, the corners of his blue eyes crinkling engagingly. "Yes, it is awful, isn't it?"

"Yassuh!" said the man, his bald head and shiny round cheeks making him look like an overgrown eight ball. Then, critical of Jack's understatement, he added: "Awful just ain't the word for it! The kitchen's in an uproar. They's all a-screeed to go to bed tonight. Maybe we-all 'll be murdered in our beds." The man's fear was tinged with pleasure at the prospect of a possible interruption in his monotonous routine.

"Don't worry," laughed Jack. "No one's going to murder you in your bed—not unless you don't get this place cleaned up properly."

"Yassuh, yassuh!" And the porter took the hint, getting back on his knees, and resuming his vigorous scrubbing.

Jack and Windy stood there looking at the bandstand. It was a shambles. The microphone still lay on the floor below, the wire which extended from it coiling away like a thing alive. The music stands, once in orderly formation, were now scattered every which way. Some had tumbled over against chairs which in turn had been overturned when the players had scrambled from their seats. Instruments had been put down hastily, some on the floor, and some on chairs, and sheets of music manuscript were scattered all over. Gone now was the precise and clean-cut arrangement of the seating. Nothing was where it should have been.

"Can't tell now where anyone was sitting, exactly," thought Jack. What a mess! He was seeing again Andy's figure slumping to the floor. And there was his chair, on the left end of the bandstand, with his own personal stand in front of it, so proudly lettered with his initials.

They walked up the steps, and saw that behind the stand, Andy's trombone had fallen off the chair where he

had so carefully placed it before going up to the microphone to sing—before going up to the microphone to die.
. . . Jack picked it up, and examined the dent on the edge
of the horn. It didn't matter now. Andy wouldn't use it
again. Andy was now lying terribly still under a sheet upstairs. Jack shook off his morbid thoughts with difficulty, and replaced the trombone on Andy's chair. He began
straightening the stand, but Windy touched his arm re-
strainingly.

"Don't, Jack," he said. "Don't touch anything you don't
have to. It's better for everything to stay just as is until the
cops get here. You know—those fingerprints—"

"That's right," acknowledged Jack, and thought about
the cops. To him, the ways of the police were mysterious. His only official contact with them to date had been
an occasional bawling out by New York's Finest, and one
speed ticket. What in the world did they do in a case like
this? Where did they start? He certainly was in a fix now!
He did remember vaguely from reading detective novels
that they took fingerprints, asked for alibis, and ham-
mered away at suspects until the murderer gave himself
away. Then they reported to Scotland Yard. No—that was
in England, wasn't it? . . . Oh, it was all so confusing. And
he was supposed to be a detective!

Windy had been staring silently at the trombone that
Jack had just replaced, thinking his own morbid thoughts.
He shook himself suddenly, like a plump puppy emerging
from a cold bath, and said: "C'mon, Jack. Let's get that
drink they were all talking about so much. I sure can use
it now. Guess I got the creeps. God! What a set-up!"

He opened the door behind the curtain, and they walked
into the lounge. Buddy, Ray, and Iggy had already preced-
ed them. They all had glasses in their hands, filled from
the bottles of whiskey on a table, with a tray of glasses
beside them. Max was there too, sitting in a corner by

himself. He was immobile, staring into space. He appeared
to be dazed.

Jack looked about the room, hardly seeing the men
there. Then he realized that he had unconsciously been
looking for Lee. But she wasn't there.

The room was silent with an uneasy, waiting silence.
Buddy was sitting on the couch, his face that of a solemn Puck. Iggy was as usual at the piano, but he was
now sitting with his back to it, as if even the reminder of
music was distasteful to him. His lean, handsome face was
moody, and there were noticeable lines of strain tracing
their way from the corners of his nostrils to his mouth.
His long fingers were playing nervously with a cigarette
lighter, lighting it, then jerking the flame out. He watched
the flame die with a brooding expression.

All the rest were sunk in some lethargy, which was dis-
pelled somewhat at the entrance of Jack and Windy into
the room.

Buddy pushed a half empty bottle toward them, and
said: "Have a drink, boys. It's on the house—I hope! Our
motto is: 'Drink, drink, and be merry, for tomorrow you—'"

A glass shattered suddenly on the floor. Everyone
jumped, startled at the unexpected sound.

Tony, sitting in an armchair, looked stupidly at the
whiskey glass which had slipped from his hand. A spot
spread itself leisurely on the red rug. A dark stain, reminiscent— Tony's olive skin looked sallow in the light, and
now he turned yellow with anger.

"Why in hell don't you keep your big trap shut, Buddy!" he snarled.

"Tsk, tsk!" answered Buddy, eyeing him insolently.
"What are *you* so nervous about, Tony?"

The door opened after a light knock, and Lee entered.
She was wearing a red quilted jacket over her bare shoulders, and her face was pale and tired-looking.

"Kitty's asleep," she announced. "But I promised to come back soon, and stay with her for the rest of the night." She sat down on the couch next to Buddy, so that she was right in Jack's line of vision. Buddy offered her a drink, but she waved it away, and some of the others helped themselves again in silence.

Frankie was at the card table by himself, playing solitaire, a nearly empty whiskey bottle at his elbow. At least he had the cards laid out for solitaire, but he wasn't concentrating on it. He picked up a card from the top of the deck, looking at it with eyes that did not see, then flung it down with a bang on the table.

"There goes a job—shot to hell!" he said bitterly. "Now what?—If we ever get out of this God-forsaken place, that is?"

"A job isn't all you have to worry about right now, dim wit," said Tony, getting up to refill his glass. "That's the least of it!"

"What are you insinuating?" asked Frankie, rising, his bony, receding jaw set in an ugly line.

"Oh, quit it, you two!" commanded Iggy. "We're all in the same boat now."

"Yes," put in Lee, the dark shadows under her eyes making them look enormous in her white face, "Iggy is right. We're all in for a bad time, at best."

"Well, look, boys," said Jack, somewhat hesitantly. "Perhaps we can straighten this out by ourselves. We'll have some time before the police get here. As Windy told you, I've—er—had some experience as a detective—" he crossed his fingers mentally at this—"and maybe we can solve this mess if everyone co-operates."

Ray stood up. "Personally," he said, speaking deliberately, "I think we should just stand pat. We'll just get excited without accomplishing anything. You may have some experience as a detective, as you say, but after all, you have no real authority."

"He's awfully conspicuous for a detective," Buddy remarked, eyeing Jack with curiosity. "Of course, he could disguise himself as a string-bean, if he dyed his freckles and that brick top green."

"I say, let the police handle this when they get here," continued Ray. "That's what they get paid for."

Jack looked at the others for co-operation, but was met for the most part by indifferent glances.

"Don't you fellows see that all of us, including me, are going to be in trouble when the police get here?" he pleaded earnestly. "We'll certainly be let in for a lot of inconvenience anyway. The evidence is of necessity circumstantial, and we'll be questioned over and over again. That is, I think it was circumstantial, unless someone saw something . . ." He glanced about the room, waiting for a reply, but nothing was said.

Then Jimmy spoke up flippantly. "It was awful dark, Mister, remember?"

"Yes, Andy's ego led to his own undoing," Iggy remarked soberly. "If he hadn't insisted on that spotlight for his solo tonight—"

They all digested this in silence for a minute then Jack shook his head in denial. "Uh-uh! I think you're wrong, Iggy. Someone hated Andy enough to shoot him, and—"

"Unless someone was just cleaning a gun, and didn't know it was loaded," suggested Buddy with an impish leer.

". . . and he would have made another opportunity if this one hadn't presented itself," continued Jack, ignoring Buddy.

"Well, I think Ray is right," said Frankie, blinking nervously. "I don't see what business this is of ours. I—I didn't kill him—and what's more, I don't care who did!"

He threw out this statement defiantly, with a challenging air. "Besides," he concluded, "maybe it was a burglar, or—or something . . ." His voice trailed off lamely, and as he poured himself another drink, his hands shook visibly.

Jack watched him for a moment, then said: "I don't mean to be presumptuous. I know I'm new here—new in fact to the whole professional music business. I don't want to be officious, or—or nosy." He spoke slowly, groping for the right words. He felt that Lee's eyes were fixed intently on him, and he flushed, then continued hastily:

"What's the use of kidding ourselves? What I'm trying to say is that Frankie's burglar just won't wash, and you know it."

"And why not?" asked Frankie belligerently.

"Could anyone have come in that door?" Jack asked, nodding in the direction of the exit from the lounge to the back of the building.

They all looked, and saw that the key was still in the lock. Jack walked over and tried the door. It held fast.

"The answer is obviously no," he continued, "because if anyone had come in through here, even if the door hadn't been locked, the floor here would be full of snow and sleet. And you can see for yourselves, it's dry. Now, how about your room, Lee?"

"There's the same kind of exit in my dressing room," Lee answered, "and that's always locked too."

"Right! And could anyone have come up the steps of the platform on either side—I mean after Max turned the lights down?"

"It is possible, I believe," said Ray, wrinkling his high forehead judiciously, as he tried to picture the scene.

"What are you talking about, Ray!" Buddy said impatiently. "Not in the dark. They'd trip over Andy's chair on his end. It was right in front of the steps, and almost against the wall. Besides, my stand is right next to Andy's chair, and I'm sure I'd have heard anyone trying to come up."

"And how about you, Iggy?" asked Jack. "Your piano is right up against the left end and facing the steps. Could anyone have come up those steps without your being aware of it? Up, and around the piano in back of the boys?"

Iggy thought about it for a moment, then shook his head decisively. "Nope! Because when Lee has a vocal to sing she has to pass around my piano to get down front to the mike from her room, and I can always tell when she does. So it wouldn't be possible for anyone to come up and around without my knowing about it. No one did, I'm positive."

"Well," continued Jack, "that eliminates all those kids, who were dancing—including Kitty and her med student, of course. That also eliminates the staff, waiters, bus boys and so forth. It eliminates Si, who was lying drunk in his room. All those people are out, definitely! So you see—" Jack's voice dropped to barely above a whisper, and the room was deathly still, with a quiet that waited—"so you see that only someone who was on the bandstand could have been responsible for what happened."

He looked carefully about the room at each individual. "In other words—*one of us is a murderer!*"

# 7

The silence was ominous. Then Buddy, who had turned pale, laughed nervously and said:

"Come on now, you naughty murderer, speak up! Whoever you are, confess!"

Jimmy snickered.

Jack rubbed his forehead in despair. Most of these boys were young, much younger than he, except for Windy. It was hopeless to make them take this affair seriously, to make them aware of the gravity of the situation.

"Look, Buddy," he said, trying to be patient. "I don't mean to criticize. I know we're upset, and high-strung. But it would help if you acted a little less like an adolescent."

"O.K.," said Buddy agreeably. "So I'll act like a suspect. Suspect music, please!" he commanded, and slunk furtively about the room, twirling an imaginary mustache, and comically rolling his eyes.

Lee giggled, and the others started laughing. Even Jack couldn't help smiling. And it did relieve the tension somewhat.

"You look a lot more like Groucho Marx than a suspect, infant," said Iggy, his face lighting up as he laughed.

"Aw shucks!" said Buddy as he sat down, satisfied with the attention he was getting. "And I thought I looked like Jerry Colonna. I am a failure!"

"Look, you!" said Tony, breaking in impatiently, and addressing Jack. "I don't like your attitude. What right have you to accuse us like that?"

"I'm not accusing anyone, yet," answered Jack. "All I said was that it was someone on the bandstand who killed Andy. That's obvious. And don't forget, I was on it with the rest of you. That means that I as well as you am suspect until the murderer is uncovered."

Tony shrugged his shoulders. "Maybe so. But don't forget that most of us were playing at the time. I play sax, if you remember, and you can't very well fire a gun while playing an instrument like that. It would take an octopus to do it. As I said, *most* of us were playing." Tony paused for emphasis, then continued with a significant nod in Max's direction: "Most of us, but not all of us."

Max had been sitting quietly, listening to the conversation, but at the manifest accusation in Tony's voice, the color drained from his face.

"Look!" said Buddy in a piercing whisper. "His face is Tattle-Tale Gray!"

Max stood up hastily, pushing his chair back with an angry movement.

"You young fool!" he yelled at Buddy. "You're always joking! You think life is just one big joke for your benefit! Even a funeral is funny to you—to all you fellers. You're all alike. Now you try to pin this thing on me!" His voice rose shrilly, and he resembled an aged gnome in a temper.

"Don't get so excited, Max," said Lee, rising and going to him. "Tony didn't mean anything, did you, Tony?"

"Oh, no?" Tony laughed mockingly. "I wasn't just talking for my health."

"I didn't do it!" screamed Max, the cords in his neck standing out conspicuously. "And you can't prove I did!"

"Please, Max, calm yourself," said Jack, distressed at the little man's all too obvious fear. "We won't get anywhere if you get so excited. Tell us what you were doing on the bandstand after you turned the spotlight on for Andy. Did you go back into the lounge?"

"No," answered Max, subsiding a little. He addressed Jack alone, feeling that he was sympathetic and willing to believe him. "I didn't go in again. I—I was standing by the electric switchbox there on the wall, and—well, I guess I was thinking about Kitty and that boy she was dancing with. You know—Butch. I was thinking that he was the right kind of feller for her—her age, her kind. And he likes her so much, too. And then I thought about Kitty's mother, and how much like her Kitty looks. And I was thinking about—about—"

"Don't be afraid to admit it, Max," said Jack, prompting him gently. "You were thinking about Andy, and his influence on your daughter, weren't you?"

Max looked down at his stubby hands.

"You see, Max," continued Jack, feeling sorry for him, "the police will find out about it anyway. You can't possibly conceal the fact that you hated Andy, and that you did have the opportunity to kill him. But that doesn't mean so much. If you're innocent, as you say you are, you aren't in danger."

"I didn't do it," insisted Max.

Jack was silent a moment, then asked him: "What did you mean by saying: 'You won't be bothering her much longer!' to Andy? I mean when you were quarreling here with him before we started playing? That sounded suspiciously like a threat. Was it?"

"Threat?" asked Max, looking nonplussed. Then his face brightened a little; "Oh, that! I know what you mean now. No, that wasn't a threat. I meant that I was sending Kitty away to college—to Michigan.

"You see, it's this way: Kitty's been living with her aunt in the city, so she could go to high school there. When she graduated, I thought she'd stay with me for a year, and then go away to college. She's all I have . . ." Max paused, his eyes dim with emotion. "And—well, she's young, and didn't have anything to do here. Andy is glamorous, and famous, so she fell for him. He was bored, and he'll go for anything in skirts that's good-looking . . . So I decided to put an end to his monkey business, and send her away at the beginning of next term; that is, in January, instead of next September. So why should I kill him?" he continued, now calmed down. "I wouldn't be such a fool. Don't you think I know what effect it would have on Kitty, even if I could get away with it? It's worse this way. Now she'll idolize Andy—make a martyr of him. You all saw how she carried on. Now she'll never forget him!" And he buried his face in his hands.

"But you did hate him just the same?" asked Ray, unmoved by this display of emotion.

"Who liked him?" Max asked pointedly. "Did you?"

"How about a gun, Max?" asked Jack. "You don't happen to have one, do you?"

"Why, yes!" answered Max, with a startled look. "Yes, I have a revolver. And I have a permit for it too," he added hastily. "We were held up once, and those bandits got away with a Saturday night's receipts, so the cops advised me to get a gun for protection. This place is so far from the main road."

"Where do you keep this revolver?"

"In the desk drawer in my office here. Wait; I'll go get it." Max got up with relief, and scurried out.

Frankie watched him disappearing through the door with a sceptical look.

"I think you guys are all screwy!" he exclaimed, reaching for another drink. "He admits he has a gun, and you let him go get it! Some detective you are! I wouldn't trust him. If you ask me, he has a screw loose—probably went nuts worrying about Kitty, and shot Andy."

"Don't be ridiculous, Frankie," commented Ray with a supercilious look. "You don't think he will come back with that revolver, do you? If he did it, he'll say it's missing anyway. Any fool would know enough to do that."

"I think you fellows have the wrong slant on Max," said Iggy, shifting restlessly on his piano stool. "I simply can't imagine him shooting someone in the back like that—in cold blood. He's—he's just not the type."

"Exactly what type do you think a murderer belongs to?" Ray asked scornfully. "A dese, dem, and dose criminal with a protruding jaw and a prizefighter's nose? That idea of the criminal type is outmoded. Anyone with sufficient provocation is capable of killing. Anyone! And that goes for all of us!"

The door was pushed open, and Max entered.

"The phone isn't working yet," he announced breathlessly. "I tried it again while I was in the office."

"What about the gun?" asked Ray with a knowing smile on his face.

"Oh, yes," said Max, reaching into his pocket. "Here it is. It was still in the drawer, just where I always keep it. It wasn't touched at all." And he took out a revolver, a shiny, deadly-looking object. Jack's only experience with guns to date had been limited to the rifles used in the firing ranges in Coney Island, but even he could see that this one was old-fashioned and unwieldy.

They all gathered around Max, inspecting it with curiosity. "Gosh," said Buddy in awe, "you could end a war with that cannon!"

Max broke it open, and displayed the cartridges, none of them used. "See," he said triumphantly. "It wasn't fired!"

Windy reached over and felt the barrel. "No, it wasn't," he confirmed. "It's still cold. Guess this wasn't the gun that killed Andy."

"Which means that someone else here had a gun—and used it!" Jack said slowly. "Better lock that revolver away, Max. And keep an eye on it."

"Yeah," said Frankie suspiciously, "but who's gonna keep an eye on Max?"

Tony spoke up. His shiny white teeth made a startling contrast to his red lips and olive complexion.

"Aren't you boys forgetting that Max wasn't the only one who had a motive as well as an opportunity?" he drawled.

"What do you mean?" asked Jack, his heart beating wildly. He felt sick. He knew what was coming, and there was no way to prevent it. His tongue went swiftly over his dry lips, as he repeated: "Whom are you referring to, Tony?"

"Come, come, now!" Tony said, narrowing his eyes until they were slits. "You all know very well whom I'm referring to. Let's not be so chivalrous, boys. After all, if we're trying to investigate a murder, we can't play favorites. The police won't, you know." He paused, but when no one spoke, he continued:

"There's one other person here who had an excellent opportunity to get on the bandstand unobserved. You spoke about the door leading to the exit from Lee's room. Weren't you forgetting that no one could have entered that way even if the door hadn't been locked, because Lee was there? Weren't you, Lee?" asked Tony, smiling—with a smile that Jack wanted terribly to smash off his face.

Lee eyed him silently.

"Or were you on the bandstand?" persisted Tony.

"I was in my room," Lee said quietly. Her eyes were smudges in her white face, and there were tiny tired lines around her mouth. The red of the jacket made her face seem more bloodless by comparison.

"But you could have come out from your room, and walked behind the band. Easily, couldn't you?" Tony asked relentlessly. "Well, couldn't you?"

"I suppose so," she answered after an instant's hesitation. "It's possible. I could have, but I didn't. Why should I have any desire to kill Andy? I didn't have anything against him."

"Not much, you didn't!" sneered Tony. "Who hasn't read that item in Winchell's column last week—the one where he mentioned that Markman of the G & O Agency had you lined up for a commercial, a solo spot—the kind of thing a vocalist would give a front tooth for? You didn't take the offer, did you? Andy was paying you thirty a week—peanuts! And Markman's offer would have netted you at least three hundred a week. So why didn't you take it?"

Lee sat up straight in the armchair, her hands closing spasmodically on its arms. Her face was expressionless, but when she spoke it was through stiff lips.

"You know very well why I couldn't take the offer. Andy had me under contract for a year. I've only been with him for three months. He promised to build my name up, give me publicity, and for the last six months of my contract, I was to get fifty a week. Even that would hardly have been enough to keep me in gowns. But I couldn't break a contract, so I had to refuse the commercial."

Jack thought he would suffocate. No, it wasn't true. She wouldn't murder. Why, the very idea was absurd.

"So you admit that Andy's death is very opportune for you," Tony went on cruelly. "Your contract with Andy is invalid now, and you're free to sign up for that commercial. And maybe your mother will be able to use the extra money for an operation. It all works out very conveniently for you—too conveniently, if you ask me."

"And who the hell asked you?" Iggy interrupted violently, unable to contain himself any longer. "What are *you* throwing all that baloney around for? You—you corny sax blower! Your nose isn't clean, either, so be careful how you go around accusing people. You're liable to wind up in your own trap, so keep it shut!"

Good for Iggy, thought Jack exultantly. He sounded as if he had something on Tony. But the saxophonist merely looked bland, and shrugged his shoulders unconcernedly. He rose to fill his glass.

"Tony," said Jack, trying hard to be fair, "Iggy seems to know something about you. Maybe you'd better tell us about it yourself."

"I haven't any idea what that guy's talking about," Tony denied after a long drink from his glass.

"Well, then, Iggy, you tell us, if he won't."

"It'll be a pleasure!" Iggy announced grimly. "A few weeks ago Andy caught Tony trying to sell the fellows in the band reefers—marijuana cigarettes. I don't have to tell you what that means. It's a federal offense. Even if Tony weren't convicted, by some chance, the union would throw him out, and he'd never be able to get a job with another band. Not a pleasant prospect—and Andy had the power to do that to Tony. And, being Andy, he probably kept Tony wriggling on the hook, wondering what would happen. So Andy's death makes it convenient for you too, eh, Tony?"

"You can't prove a thing," said Tony casually, not at all disturbed by the accusation. "And if you're through telling those tall tales, you long drink of poison, I have another contribution to make to our fund of information:

"You see, Mr. Detective," he continued with a mocking glance at Jack, "Iggy's nose, as he so charmingly puts it, isn't clean either. It happens that our budding genius, right here, is the actual composer of *Headlined in My Heart,* the song now occupying a prominent position on the Hit Parade. In other words, contrary to the credit line on the sheet music, Andy did not write it. So make something out of that!"

Iggy's face turned dark. He swung around violently on the stool, and began playing dissonant chords on the piano, savagely striking jangling noise.

Jack was shocked. And he had thought Andy such a wonderful composer! How was it possible that Iggy should have let him take the credit for it?

"Stop, Iggy!" he said loudly, trying to make himself heard above the banging discords. "Iggy! Listen to me, please!"

Iggy stopped bearing down on the keyboard, but sat as he was, facing the piano.

"Tell me what happened. How come Andy has his name on the song when you're the one who really wrote it?" Jack asked.

Iggy swung around again, his face expressionless, his features under control, except for his mouth, which was a thin bitter line.

"All right!" he admitted somberly. "So I wrote it. So what?"

"Then why isn't your name on it?" persisted Jack.

"Well, after I wrote it, I kind of liked it, so I took it around to a couple of publishers. But they weren't having any—said it was a little fantastic—not commercial enough . . . They were just interested in corn. So I stopped bothering with it. Then I was playing the tune a few months ago, and Andy happened to overhear it. He asked me what it was, and when I told him it was mine, but that the publishers weren't interested, he offered to take it to a publisher friend of his, and to help me get it published."

"Ha!" scoffed Buddy. "Imagine Andy doing someone a good turn! Iggy, ma fran', you sure are gullible!"

"Gullible is right! Like a damned fool, I believed him. I knew he could have it plugged, so the tune wouldn't die out without a chance. So he had it published—with his name on it. After that it was too late to do anything about it. And anyway, what could I do about it? Sue him?"

"But he just couldn't get away with it!" exclaimed Jack, horrified.

"Oh, couldn't he?" Iggy asked, smiling wryly. "But he did."

"The copyright laws—what are they for?"

"I didn't bother copyrighting it—too much trouble. Anyway, copyrighting an unpublished song is an amateur custom. So you see, I can't prove a thing."

"At least you proved one thing, though," said Buddy, loyally. "The publishers were wrong about the tune not being commercial. The royalties on the records alone cleaned up a healthy young fortune."

"Yeah," said Iggy, "but Andy would have claimed it was only because his name was on it."

"So there's another motive for you," said Tony triumphantly. "And don't forget that Andy was shot while he was singing *Headlined in My Heart*. Bang! Right in the middle!"

"I don't see it," disagreed Jack. "After all, Tony, that song's been out for a few months now. So why would Iggy wait so long to get revenge?"

"Because it happens that last week Iggy's girl ran off with some press agent that she thought would be able to give her all the things she hoped to become accustomed to. Iggy's song hit the jackpot—and why shouldn't it?—it's good enough," Tony admitted grudgingly. "So if he had been cutting in on the royalties, he would have had plenty of dough coming to him. And if Andy had given him that money, maybe she'd have come back to him. Money like that is good enough bait for any skirt. And he's damn fool enough to want her back on any terms—that redheaded little tart. . . ."

But with a smothered sound of rage, Iggy was on his feet. He reached Tony before anyone could intervene, and with one blow sent him crashing to the floor!

# 8

"This fighting's getting monotonous," said Windy to Jack a short time later, with a bored look on his chubby face. "I should have brought boxing gloves along for some exercise. There are plenty of sparring partners around here."

They had managed to pull Iggy off Tony, but it had taken the combined efforts of most of the band. In the interim, Tony had acquired a cut lip and a bruised jaw in spite of their speedy intervention, and now he was sitting sullenly by himself, holding another drink.

Lee had jumped up with the others at the start of the altercation. Now she had pulled Iggy to a seat by her side on the couch, and was talking to him in a low voice. Seeing them in intimate discussion, Jack felt a momentary pang of envy.

Tony finished the drink in his glass, and started for another from the nearly depleted bottle.

"Cut it out, Tony," advised Jimmy, the second trumpeter. "You're drinking too much."

"Mind your own business!" snapped Tony. "I'll drink as much as I please!"

"Well, my fine sleuth," said Ray, his sharp nose raised triumphantly, "I told you what would happen if you started this investigation—plenty of trouble! This affair is entirely too personal to talk about calmly. And what did you discover for your pains? Nothing!"

"You're wrong, Ray," Jack answered the first saxophonist. "We've got some motives. And so far, nearly everyone
seems to have hated Andy."

"Yeah," chimed in Buddy. "Hating Andy was our favorite indoor sport. What else could we do for excitement in
this retreat from civilization?"

"Well, you're included in the bunch, Buddy," said Jack.
"Why did you dislike him?"

Buddy looked down at the untouched drink in his
hand. "Just on general principles, I guess," he answered
slowly. "And he kept picking on my playing just to annoy
me. Every time something went wrong with the tone of the
ensemble, he'd blame me for it. Even if he hit a sour note
himself, it was my fault. And I knew, too, what he'd done
to Iggy—with the song, I mean. You can't like a guy when
he does something like that."

Buddy was loyal, all right, thought Jack. Loyal, and
an idealist into the bargain. And he worshipped Iggy. But
what kind of a motive was that?

"This whole thing is screwy!" said Frankie, scratching
his head peevishly. "Max says he didn't do it; Lee says she
didn't do it. None of us could have done it—we were all
playing, and as Tony said before, we aren't octopuses—er
—octo—er—"

"You mean octopussies," said Buddy, trying to be helpful. "And their babies are called octo-kittens."

"Oh, shut up, you stale joke-book!" said Frankie irritably. "The fact remains that when I play my drums I use
both hands and my foot. So how could I fire a gun, even
if I had one, even if I knew how to fire the darn thing?
That goes for the rest of the band, too. So where does that
leave us?"

"Wait a minute!" Buddy shouted suddenly. "Maybe
someone rigged up some sort of contraption on the bandstand—in the wall, I mean—and attached it to a clock that

fired a gun while he was playing, so it would give him an alibi—or something like that . . . Anyway, let's go see!" He suited the action to his words, and with a bound he was out of the door.

The others acted on the suggestion with relief. At least it meant action of some sort, and anything was better than sitting around throwing accusations. Jack wanted to laugh at the picture of the boys looking for a complicated Rube Goldberg sort of device. But after all, Andy had been killed by a gun, and it had to be somewhere. Perhaps the murderer had left it on the bandstand. It couldn't do any harm to look.

The boys congregated on the bandstand. They avoided looking at the stains on the floor below, still visible in spite of the forceful scrubbing by the porter. They moved about aimlessly, uncertain of where to begin searching.

Jack parted the curtains, and saw that the wall all along was solid. There was no sign of Buddy's hypothetical device—no clock, no mechanical contraption, no automatic trigger. And there was nothing on the floor of the bandstand, except what should normally have been there: instrument cases, instruments, sheet music that had fallen from the racks . . .

Jack straightened up from the floor. How about the mike? Of course, Andy had been shot from behind, so nothing could have been accomplished by tampering with the mike. Still, there might be some clue there. He looked toward the center of the bandstand where the mike ordinarily stood. It had still been on the floor below when the man was cleaning, but it had been replaced now.

Someone was standing there, his back to Jack, holding the stem just the way Andy usually did when singing. . . . A figure in a tux—a figure with Andy's build—of Andy's height—and the way the hair at the nape of the neck grew—

Jack's scalp prickled.

He moved forward slowly, swallowing, his mouth dry.

The figure turned around. It *was* Andy! No, it wasn't.

"What's the matter?" asked the apparition in an earthly voice. "Don't you feel well?"

Jack's first attempt at speaking resulted in a strangled sound. Then suddenly things resolved themselves again, and he recognized the person before him.

It was Jimmy.

"Hey!" cried the second trumpeter, looking alarmed. "You don't look so hot—kinda pale. What's wrong with you, huh?"

Jack finally regained the use of his voice, "I thought— well, you looked just like Andy standing there at the mike, and for a minute I had an awful shock. I was sure it was Andy. You have the same build, same height, and your hair is exactly the same color . . ."

"What's so strange about that?" Jimmy asked with a good-natured grin. "Andy is my brother."

"Your brother?" Jack asked incredulously.

"My half-brother, to be exact. We had the same father. Andy's mother was my father's first wife. Andy is—er— was much older than I."

Jack looked at Jimmy more carefully, and this time, more sanely. There was a marked resemblance between the two, not so much of feature as of cast. It was as if Andy's face had been a sharply defined wax image, and Jimmy's was the same image after it had blurred a little.

The latter's face was rounder, the nostrils not so flaring, the mouth fuller and softer, and the chin less pugnaciously sharp. His hair was the same color, as Jack had remarked, but it was thicker, and more unruly, and not so carefully waved. The resemblance was definitely there, if you looked for it. Jack remembered now that Buddy hadn't mentioned Jimmy's last name when he had introduced the young second trumpet player.

"I guess this isn't so pleasant for you, Jimmy," he said hesitantly. "After all, if he was your brother, you must feel—"

Jimmy's face turned hard. "If you mean that old cliché about blood being thicker than water, and all that baloney, you can forget about it," he said. "You can't pick your relatives—they're wished on you whether you like 'em or not. But that doesn't mean you have to like them. Andy didn't give a damn for me, and vice versa. In fact, I saw practically nothing of him until I joined up with the band about six months ago. Andy wasn't a philanthropist in giving me the job, either. He only hired me after I was picked as one of the up and coming horn players by one of the magazine polls. So don't worry about my being sensitive about his—er—his popularity around here."

Some character, that Andy, thought Jack. Even his own brother disliked him.

"What were you doing here at the mike?" he asked.

"It was still on the floor, so I picked it up and put it back on the stand where it belongs," answered Jimmy. A sheepish expression flashed across his face. "You see, I was wondering if maybe I could sing, too—like Andy could. I was just holding the mike the way Andy did. As a matter of fact, I'd probably have started singing into it if you hadn't come up behind me like that. Here—I'd better turn the mike off."

"Let's see it," Jack said, bending over it. He raised it and lowered it, manipulating it every which way. But the silver ball was an ordinary one. There was no device or attachment that by any stretch of the imagination could have fired a gun into Andy's back.

He contemplated the boys still hunting assiduously for a gun. "There's only one thing that could have happened," he said to Jimmy. "Someone had a gun in his hand, and shot Andy with it. The Rube Goldberg contraption of Buddy's is nonsense. We're just wasting our time."

"Hey, Windy!" he called. "Find anything?"

"What do you think?" asked Windy, righting a chair with a disgusted scowl, and coming over to them. "There's no gun around here. If you ask me, I think Buddy's throwing us a red herring just for the fun of it. Just look at him, will ya?"

Buddy was crawling around on his hands and knees, his right hand clutching an imaginary magnifying glass. He peered seriously, through it at the chairs, at the floor, and at anything that happened to be in his way. When he noticed that most of the others had stopped to watch him, his antics became more reminiscent of a musical comedy sleuth.

"What are you doing, Buddy?" asked Ray, exasperated.

Buddy's face assumed an expression of injured innocence. "I'm looking for clues. I'm the old clues man. Any old clues today . . . ? Button, button, who's got the clue? Fingerprints, torn letters, get them here! Cigarette butts. . . . Say!" He stared at something on the floor, his face portentous. "Who smokes Chesterfields?"

"I do!" admitted Frankie, with a startled movement. "Why?"

"Gimme one, huh?" said Buddy, grinning. "I'm all out of them."

Frankie handed him the package with relief. "That clowning's gonna get you in dutch some day, you crazy kid," he said, blinking his eyes in that familiar way.

"Well, anyway, it made me hungry," said Buddy, helping himself to a handful of cigarettes from the pack. "I sure could stand some nourishment."

Then Jack realized that he too had a hollow feeling in the pit of his stomach. He had mistaken it for apprehension, but it was simply good old-fashioned hunger. It seemed like years since he had last eaten—in Child's that was, in Times Square—before he had joined up with this wacky bunch.

The others were in accord. "God knows we have plenty of stuff left," grumbled Max. "No customers to eat tonight, so you fellers may as well have the benefit. I'll tell the cook to prepare some fresh coffee and sandwiches. How's that?"

A chorus of "Swell!" and "Don't forget the pickles!" and "No mustard on mine!" trailed after him as he rolled down the steps and headed for the kitchen. The group broke up then and headed once more for the lounge.

"Say, Jack," said Windy in a low voice, "I'm not much on this detection business, but how about the orchestration?"

"What do you mean?"

"Well, Tony said everyone was playing when Andy was killed. The orchestration ought to tell us exactly what each player was doing at the time, and who had an opportunity, even if it was only for a moment."

"Maybe," said Jack thoughtfully. "It won't do any harm to examine the orchestration carefully." He and Windy gathered all the instrument parts for *Headlined in My Heart* from the music racks, and took them inside. The others looked curiously at the manuscripts in their hands.

"It's the orchestration," he explained. "Windy thought it might give us some sort of clue."

They crowded around him. "Let's see now," Jack said as he thumbed through the sheets. "Andy was shot just as he was finishing the middle of the first chorus, the release, right? He was on the word 'and' that starts the last eight bars of the chorus. And look!" he exclaimed. "Andy sings that measure solo. In other words, when he was singing the word, 'and,' no instrument was playing."

"That's right!" confirmed Ray, peering over Jack's shoulder at the manuscripts. "The band ends the obbligato on the down beat, and Andy comes in alone on the upbeat immediately afterward."

"Which leaves the whole business open," remarked Windy, looking about the room at large. "No one is eliminated."

Just then Max entered, followed by a waiter wheeling in a serving table.

"Food, beautiful food!" exclaimed Buddy, and started grabbing. "Goody, I'm famished! Help yourself, boys!" he directed grandly, his mouth full. "It'll give you a vacation from our sleuth here. I can see that gleam in his eye that means another inquisition."

Jack laughed as he helped himself to a roast beef sandwich. "Oh, come now, Buddy, I'm not that bad. I'm just curious, that's all."

"Nosy, they call it in my country." But Buddy's words were bantering.

Jack watched him cutting up as usual. There didn't seem to be any real harm in him, unless— There it was! Someone in the room was a killer, and everyone was suspect. Everyone, even me, thought Jack. Maybe they suspect me, even though I never saw Andy before in my life. Not that I can blame them. After all, what do they know about Windy and me?

Lee was sitting on the couch, with a plate of sandwiches on her lap and a cup of hot, fragrant coffee in her hand, brought to her by the ever-attentive Iggy. There was an empty seat on the couch beside her, and Jack, taking his own food, hastened over to her.

"Hello!" she welcomed him with a smile. "Filling your inner man satisfactorily?"

Iggy was on her other side, nibbling at a sandwich, and smoking between bites.

"Say, Jack," he asked, "what do you think of this idea? I mean about the instruments not being in use when Andy was shot. I don't think—"

"Boys, boys!" said Lee in mock despair. "Can't we have just a few moments respite from that depressing subject? Here we are, snowbound in a blizzard; the telephone wires are down; a murder has been committed; everyone is suspected, including me; say, this hasn't been at all a pleasant evening! So can't we have a few minutes intermission? Take five, as the boys say—please?"

"You're right, Lee," agreed Iggy with a dazzling smile at her. "The others seem to have the same idea." He nodded at the rest of the band and Max, who had gathered around the card table with their steaming cups of coffee, and were busily engaged in swapping yarns.

"The boys are deep in an intellectual pursuit," laughed Lee. "Dirty stories, no doubt."

At that moment, Buddy called out: "Hey, Iggy! Come here and tell Windy that one about the Eskimo and the chorus girl."

Nothing loath, Iggy rose, and said: "You take care of Lee for a while. I'm wanted in the entertainment division."

"It'll be a pleasure!" Jack said heartily.

He glanced at Windy, noting his cherubic face now creased with laughter. They could all have had so much fun, if it had only turned out differently. Jack thought wistfully. Now, who knew what would happen after tonight? He and Windy would be looking for other jobs. . . .

"Penny for your thoughts," said Lee with an oblique glance at him. "Are you wishing you were hearing all about the Eskimo and the chorus girl instead of sitting here with me? You're perfectly free to join them if you want to."

"Oh, no!" Jack said hastily. "I wasn't thinking of that at all. I'd much rather be with you, honestly I would."

"Then what were you thinking about so earnestly? Your forehead looked as if it had just been freshly plowed."

"I'm afraid I was thinking about that taboo subject," admitted Jack, "and what it would mean when—"

"Yes." Her face turned serious; her gray eyes were hidden by those incredibly long lashes. "They may as well enjoy themselves now."

"Andy caused an awful lot of unhappiness," Jack mused. "Of course, you can't exactly blame him for Iggy's bad luck with his girl, but look at the unhappiness that was in store for Kitty; temporarily anyway."

"Kitty will never know just how lucky she is," Lee said gravely. "I know she has a childish tendency to dramatize everything, but I think she really was crazy about Andy."

"Isn't it possible that Andy intended to play square with her?" argued Jack. "She said that they were engaged. Maybe Andy was serious about her."

"That wolf?" Lee asked skeptically. "Impossible! The only person Andy could ever have cared for seriously was Andy Parker!"

"Well, anyway," argued Jack, "I don't see that Andy could have done her so much harm. She'd probably have found out for herself, eventually, that he wasn't any good. She'd have gotten over him."

"You think so?" asked Lee with a half smile. "You evidently don't know very much about love."

"O.K., Doris Blake," laughed Jack. "You tell me all about it."

"Look at Iggy," she said, refusing to fall in with his banter. "Tony was nasty about his girl, but it just happens that he was right. She wasn't any good, not one tenth good enough for Iggy, and don't you think he knows it? Of course he does! But he can't help himself. He's still crazy about her, and he's not the type to get over things easily. He'd take her back in a minute, if she'd come."

"So you think Kitty wouldn't have forgotten about Andy if he'd lived?" asked Jack. "Not even if she found out what a rat he was?"

"Andy had a terrific drag for some women," Lee answered. "I see you don't believe me. Well, just to prove I'm right, I'll tell you about Rosanne Abbott."

"I was hoping you would. It's strange that her death wasn't publicized."

"Not so strange when you know about it." Lee glanced at the group around the card table. The air above them was thick with cigarette smoke, but they were happily engaged in their story telling, and oblivious to everything else. Buddy was holding forth in dialect with the latest Lapidus story.

"As you know, Rosanne sang with the band before I did," said Lee, certain of not being interrupted. "When I signed up with Andy, I knew nothing about her, except that she had left the band rather abruptly. I got the job through an agency, and I was glad to get it. But I was rather curious at her reason for leaving, because she just disappeared from sight, instead of going with another band, as would ordinarily have happened.

"Then one day, after I'd been singing with Andy for about a month, I got a phone call from Rosanne. She wanted me to come to see her—said she had something important to tell me. Naturally, I went.

"She had a room in a cheap little hotel off Broadway, and—well, she looked a mess. She'd let herself go completely. She asked me lots of questions, about how Andy behaved with me, whether he was fresh, and—oh, you know." Lee flushed, then continued: "He had bothered me at first, but stopped when I made it clear to him exactly how I felt. It was just no dice as far as I was concerned. I know he's attractive, and practically irresistible to most women, but he didn't register with me.

"I told Rosanne so, and she said I was lucky, because Andy had ruined her life. She talked wildly, and then

showed me a picture that was on her dresser. It was a candid shot of her and a man—her ex-husband, she said it
was. I'd never seen him before, and she didn't say anything
more about him. I didn't know she was married, but singers very often do keep their marriages secret, because of
the possible effect it might have on their popularity.

"She didn't give me much more information, just warned
me again to keep away from Andy, and to get another job
when my contract ran out. Then she got hysterical, and
began screaming for me to get out."

Lee put her hand over her eyes. It was difficult for her
to continue.

"I'll never forget how she looked that day," she finally
went on in a husky voice. "She was really very pretty—
looked surprisingly like Kitty, only a little older, of course,
with blonde hair, big baby blue eyes, a small cupid's bow
mouth—or, you know the type—"

"Yes, I know what she looked like," said Jack. "I saw her
in a movie short Andy made while she was still with him."

"Well, you should have seen her then! Sitting there in
that miserable little hole, looking nearer forty than twenty, in a dirty old wrapper, her hair uncombed, her eyes
bloodshot, not a bit of make-up—just like an old hag!"
Lee shuddered at the remembrance.

After a moment she continued: "I couldn't get her out
of my mind somehow, and a few days later, when I was
in town to see my folks, I went back to see her, to see if
I could help her. But the clerk at the hotel said she was
gone, and wouldn't tell me where. I flirted a little with
him—I did so want to know where she had gone—and the
clerk finally broke down and told me she had committed
suicide—had taken poison. She had been registered under
another name, but Andy must have found out about it,
because he managed to keep it out of the papers. He had
enough influence . . ."

"But why did she leave the band if she was so crazy about Andy?" Jack asked.

"She had a year's contract, just like mine, and when the year was up, Andy didn't renew it. He was through with her, and made no bones about it. At least that's what I gathered. Rosanne didn't speak very coherently." Lee's eyes darkened at the memory. "I think that the reason she got in touch with me was that she was jealous, and not to warn me for my own benefit." Lee smiled a bitter, twisted smile. "What do they say? There, but for the grace of God, go I!"

"Don't feel so badly about it, Lee," Jack tried to comfort her. "She probably would have done it eventually anyway. If she was weak, and couldn't take it, the fault lay in her own character."

"Platitudes, platitudes!" Lee exclaimed impatiently.

"All right," Jack said hastily. "But don't get mad, please."

"I'm not." And Lee smiled to prove it. "It's just that whoever killed Andy did the world a favor."

"And how!" agreed Jack. "But I still say that murder is a crime, and as such is punishable."

"You're very self-righteous, aren't you!" mocked Lee.

"No, I'm not!" Jack protested. "I'm just an ordinary law-abiding American—I like swing, baseball, and corn on the cob. I sing in the shower, play a bad game of golf—"

"And mouth vague syllables when you sing *The Star Spangled Banner*," Lee finished for him.

"But I insist that justice means the punishment of criminals as well as the protection of the innocent," Jack insisted stubbornly. "And if a murderer isn't a criminal, who is?"

"Oh, I suppose you're right," Lee said, and then yawned, "I'm not bored," she laughed in apology, "This emotional spree has worn me out. I think I'd better see how Kitty is." And she rose.

Lee walked over to the Venetian blind covering the window and peered through it at the storm raging outside.

The group at the card table had broken up into smaller groups. Frankie was trying to persuade some of them to form a card game, but no one was interested. Buddy was with Iggy as usual; Ray was flipping the pages of a magazine, blinking his eyes sleepily; and Tony, Windy, and Max were listening to a late news broadcast.

Buddy observed Lee at the window, and called out: "Sister Ann, Sister Ann—are they coming?"

"No." She turned and laughed. "But that storm isn't going, either."

"I'm certainly glad that this place is built so solidly," said Ray, looking up from his magazine, and rubbing at his eyes under their glasses.

"You bet it is!" said Max, the pride shining from his round face. "No flimsy construction in this building. I had it built to specification. Solid throughout!"

"Well, I guess we won't blow away tonight," said Windy, getting up and yawning. "Hey, Jack, how about hitting the hay? I'm tired as hell!"

The others rose with one accord. Jack walked to the door with Lee, preoccupied with his failure to have accomplished anything. They walked in silence, Lee taken up with her own thoughts. The rest of the group trailed behind.

"Excuse me, Lee, for just a minute," Jack said, stopping suddenly. "I'm going back for that orchestration." She yawned again, unashamedly, and nodded in acknowledgment.

The orchestration was lying in the lounge where it had been flung carelessly with the other manuscripts, on the table. As Jack picked it up, he suddenly felt one of those unaccountable unreasoning flashes of something half remembered, but it returned to his subconscious as quickly as it had come. He tried desperately to regain that exhilarating sensation of omniscience, but he was trying too hard. Did it have something to do with the orchestration in his hand? Did he know something vital to the solution of this mystery? He rubbed his head with irritation, trying to concentrate. Oh, what was the use! It was sometimes difficult to recall something you knew, the name of a friend, for instance, and in this case, he didn't even know what it was he was trying to remember. Well, let it go. Perhaps it would pop into his mind when he least expected it.

Jack left the lounge, and found that the others had gone, all but Windy.

"Lee went to the hotel with Max," said Windy with a smile as he noted Jack's disappointment. "I know that old slogan about accepting no substitutes, but you're stuck with me anyhow."

"You're O.K., Windy," said Jack affectionately as they walked down the steps. "I know that the others think I'm crazy, but you—even if you think so, you don't mention it. Thanks."

"Oh, I'm in on it with you," said Windy seriously. Then he smiled wryly. "After all, I got you into it, and besides, I was on that bandstand too. A police investigation won't be very pleasant for any of us when the papers get wind of it."

"That's right," said Jack. "Andy was an outstanding figure in the music world, with all the usual rig-a-ma-gig: fan clubs, press agents, publicity set-ups. The jitterbugs alone will raise holy hell! And the sob sisters and reporters will tear every one of us to pieces, have a Roman holiday on us. Every paper will be trying to beat the police to the solution, so that they'll have a scoop, as well as the opportunity to say: 'N'ya, n'ya, ya dumb bunnies,' to the police. Gosh, what a prospect!"

"And if the police don't uncover the murderer—and they don't always—it'll mean that we'll all have plenty of trouble getting another job. An agency won't take a chance on recommending a possible murderer, or even someone who's notorious. And that's just what we'll be when they get through with us."

"You don't have to worry about that, Windy," Jack reassured him. "Not a musician with your reputation and ability. After all, they don't find clarinetists like you on the street!"

Windy's chubby face looked stubborn. "Maybe so, but mark my words, it won't be so pleasant for any of us."

"O.K., you pessimist," laughed Jack, "You'll feel better after a good night's sleep."

"I guess so." Windy yawned. "Am I tired! Say, do you snore?"

"I wouldn't know," laughed Jack. "I sleep too soundly to wake myself up."

"Well, as long as you don't wake me up—" And Windy opened the door to their room.

# 9

They started undressing, but Jack was too full of what had happened to be quiet for long. He went to the dresser and picked up the orchestration.

"Look, Windy," he said, looking through the parts again. "You're a good musician. You ought to know what a player can do while he's playing his instrument. How could any of the boys have had a chance to pick up a gun, or take it out of his pocket, or wherever he had concealed it, then aim, and fire—all in the second just before Andy came in? Andy held the word 'dreams' for four beats, and during them, every one of the band had a part to play. It isn't logical—physically impossible, in fact."

"Well, impossible or not, someone did it," said Windy, pursing his lips judiciously. "Unless of course it was either Max, or— O.K., O.K.! I didn't mean it. You don't have to look as if I'd killed your grandmother."

"I don't think Max did it, and I'm positive that Lee didn't," Jack said shortly, and turned to the orchestration again.

"I said I didn't mean it," Windy said with a placating smile. "So it's one of the boys. And you're the one who says it's impossible."

"Oh, I don't know what's possible any more," Jack said irritably. "This thing is getting me down."

It was no use—the murderer needed more than one beat. Jack went over the piano sheets, the part that Iggy played in the arrangement. Just octaves in the bass during those measures with chords played by the right hand on alternate beats were written in—basic writing for a piano part. Could Iggy have played them all with his left hand, and while playing, fired with his right? Jack tried to visualize it. Oh, the very idea was absurd, because when Iggy played, he had his back to Andy, which meant that Iggy would have had to twist completely around, while playing with his left hand and aiming with his right. Possible, perhaps, but highly improbable.

If Andy had only stayed in one position while he sang, it might have been possible to tell from which direction the shot had come; but the way he twisted his body made that fact impossible to deduce.

He watched Windy open the door to the bathroom with unseeing eyes. Almost immediately, Windy's head popped around the doorway again.

"Pssst! Hey, Jack!" he called in a piercing whisper. "C'm here a minute. Hurry!"

Jack entered the bathroom hastily. Windy was listening at the other door, the one that led to the adjoining bedroom. Jack followed suit, and put his own ear to the door. Loud voices were clearly audible. An argument was evidently in progress.

". . . And you needn't act so innocent," a voice said sharply. "You had plenty to gain by Andy's death!"

"Tony!" muttered Windy. "That guy's at it again!" The other voice came back, lower, but just as clearly: "Maybe you know just how much? Andy never confided in me, and he didn't bother showing me his bank book!"

"That's Jimmy," whispered Jack. "I guess Tony is referring to the fact that Jimmy is Andy's heir."

"Heir?" asked Windy, puzzled. "What do you mean?"

"Jimmy is Andy's half-brother," answered Jack, "and unless Andy specifies otherwise in his will, most of Andy's money will go to him. Unless, of course, there are closer relatives surviving."

Windy whistled, his eyebrows going up in amazement. Then he put his ear against the door again.

". . . And Andy has plenty of money, no doubt. You get it all, don't you?"

"I don't know anything about it!" Jimmy denied vehemently. "It's true that I'm his nearest relative, but how do I know just how much money Andy left? It's true that he made a lot, but he probably spent most of it. Anyhow, just because there'll be some money coming my way doesn't mean you can pin this thing on me!"

"Oh, no?" Jack could visualize the animal-like baring of Tony's white teeth. "You had more than money to gain by Andy's death."

"I don't know what you mean." Jimmy's voice sounded frightened.

"Don't play innocent, now!" Tony said triumphantly. "You know damn well what I mean. That check—!"

Jimmy's voice shook as he answered quickly: "I don't know what you're talking about! You don't know a thing . . ."

"You forged a check with Andy's name on it, didn't you?" Tony accused him. "That means jail. Andy found out about it. It was just for a small amount, but that wasn't the reason why Andy didn't prosecute. Nor was it from any feelings of brotherly love, either. That wasn't like Andy, He kept the check so he could have a hold over you—something to make you squirm. Typically Andy. He knew all the refinements of cruelty . . ."

"Andy didn't tell you—he wouldn't! How do you know?" Jimmy was badly frightened.

Tony hesitated, then replied:

"I saw it among his things yesterday. He had the check here with him, and he wasn't clever enough to conceal it carefully."

"And what were you doing in his room?" Jimmy asked scornfully. "That sounds like you aren't in the clear, either."

Tony laughed, a sound that grated.

"Who is, here?" he mocked. "I was looking for something on him, just to give him a taste of his own medicine, so he wouldn't do anything about the reefers . . ."

"You're not much better than Andy was. Of all the dirty, underhanded snoopers!"

"Come, now, Jimmy! Calling names isn't going to help you. We're no longer children. I just thought I'd let you know about it. The police will find the check when they search Andy's room . . . !"

"Is the check still there?"

"You underestimate me, my friend," Tony said in an amused voice. "I have the check now. But when the police get there, it will be back where I found it, in Andy's room, unless—" Tony paused suggestively.

"O.K., spill it. What do you want?"

"Well," Tony drawled, "you can't make me believe that Andy didn't leave plenty of money and property. It all belongs to you now. I have something you want, and you'll soon have something I want. So if we get together on this—we'll both have a lot to gain. How about it?"

"Oh, I get it!" Jimmy raised his voice angrily; then, regaining his caution, he lowered it again. "So you're trying a little blackmail on the side!"

"The kid's intelligent!" laughed Tony. "But please let's not use such hard terms. Suppose we call it—an exchange? Of course I'll keep the check. You'll merely be buying my silence."

"So you can bleed me dry?" Jimmy asked bitterly. "I'll see you in hell before you get a cent out of me! I didn't kill Andy, so I'm not afraid of your threats, you—!" Tony interrupted him, speaking calmly and in a leisurely fashion:

"You got out of this fix pretty well. Andy can't testify against you, so you're safe on that little matter. Besides which you fall heir to a nice fat bank account and some valuable property. All in all, very satisfactory for you— ver-y satisfactory—suspiciously so!"

"I didn't kill him!" Jimmy cried hysterically. "You know too damn much for your own good, Tony! You know everything about everyone here. Maybe you know who did kill Andy!"

"Maybe I do," Tony agreed coolly. "Maybe I do! But that has nothing to do with you and me now. I'm warning you—better play ball with me—or else—" Tony's voice was grim with finality.

They could hear him starting for the bathroom door, and Windy pulled Jack back hastily into their room. They shut the door softly.

"Whew!" exclaimed Jack, folding his long legs as he sank into an armchair. "Andy certainly never read Dale Carnegie's book. He could have given anyone lessons on how to alienate people!"

"What a crew we fell in with!" Windy agreed in disgust. "That Tony's no angel, either." He scratched his thinning brown hair thoughtfully, and said:

"Say, do you think Tony could have been the one who killed Andy?"

"It's possible, of course," said Jack. "But even if he did have what seems to be an adequate motive, I think he's more the kind to limit himself to blackmail. Like that little scene we just overheard, for instance. The whole trouble is that we have motives enough, but no opportunities. I'm so darned mixed up!"

"Well, what about what Tony said just now?" Windy asked after a pause, "Do you think Jimmy would have done it?"

"That's what I'm trying to tell you, Windy," explained Jack wearily. "I don't see how *any* of them could have done it. I heard the trumpets playing sustained half notes in harmony—get it?—in harmony! That means there were two trumpets playing, which lets Jimmy out. If they were playing, as were the rest of the boys, they couldn't have fired a gun. The whole band was playing, except during that one beat rest, and that wouldn't have been time enough. . . ."

"Well, don't worry about it so much," Windy interrupted sympathetically. "Maybe the police will be able to tell what it's all about by means of the bullet and so forth . . ."

"But *I* want to do it!" Jack insisted stubbornly. "It always sounds so easy in books. Just get a bunch of clues, deduce the murderer from those clues, and then stage a reconstruction scene under the same conditions as when the crime was committed, so that the criminal will give himself away. Then you confound everyone with a brilliant and logical deduction."

"While you say: 'Element'ry, my deah people!'" laughed Windy.

"The only trouble is that I have no clues—only a bunch of motives!" Jack concluded in despair.

"None of the boys seem to care very much who the murderer is," Windy observed, as he struggled with his tie. "Maybe they're all in on it—what do you call it?—accessories."

"Could be!" Jack agreed gloomily. Then his thoughts went off in another direction.

"Say, Windy, did you know what happened to Rosanne Abbott?"

"Who's she?" asked Windy, going to the closet and hanging up his jacket.

"She was Andy's vocalist before Lee joined up with him. Lee just told me that she committed suicide."

"Yeah?" Windy's voice came back muffled from the depths of the closet. "Too bad. How come?"

"Well, Lee didn't know very much about it. You see, she visited the girl, and it happened to be just before Rosanne killed herself. She told Lee some wild story—accused Andy of ruining her life, and told Lee to beware of the big bad wolf. Lee saw her in the very same room in which she killed herself—the day before she did it, too. I wonder if there was any truth in her story. You know, sometimes girls get funny ideas and blame some guy for everything."

"With Andy, anything was possible," commented Windy. "And that certainly sounds typical of Andy's work. 's too bad. Oh, well," he said, dismissing the subject with a yawn, "I'm going to hit the hay. Mind if I use the bathroom first?"

"No, go ahead." And Jack yawned in company with Windy.

He finished undressing, got into his pajamas, and discovered that he was even wearier than he had realized. He yawned again, decided not to brush his teeth, and fell into bed.

# 10

That banging—so incessant, so irregular, and so *loud!* Why didn't somebody stop that hammering, and let a guy sleep?

Jack struggled up from the depths of his deep slumber. He lay there in the comfortable warmth, and let consciousness ooze over him, penetrating his conscious mind slowly, like a largo movement.

After an eternity of this vegetation, he found he had enough energy to open one eye, which he did, rather tentatively.

The place was strange and unfamiliar. What was he doing there? And where was his aunt who should have been waking him up?

Then, like an unexpected splash of cold water, it all came back to him with a rush. He opened the other eye and sat up quickly.

The window shade had been drawn outside the open window by the wind, and was banging away outside. That was the noise that had wakened him.

Then he saw Windy, sitting in his bathrobe, reading a newspaper, oblivious to the protesting window shade and the freezing temperature of the room.

"Hey, you Eskimo!" Jack called, burrowing under the bedclothes. "Why don't you shut the ventilation off? What do you think this is—an air-cooled movie in the summer?"

"Good morning." Windy looked up with a smile. He arose obligingly and pulled in the shade, shutting the window.

Jack yawned leisurely. "What time is it?"

"My watch is on the table here," said Windy. "Take a look," he invited.

"I forgot to wind mine last night," said Jack, reaching over for Windy's gold Bulova. "Gosh, was I tired! I slept like a log. Oh, nuts! It's only nine o'clock!"

"Middle of the night, eh?" laughed Windy. "Grab yourself some more shut-eye, why don't you?"

"It's not a bad idea! I've got that pooped-out feeling. Guess I had too much to drink last night. How come you're up so early, and where did you get that newspaper?"

"It's yesterday's," answered Windy. "I had it in my coat pocket when I drove up with you. I figure that I can read it again today, and it won't make so much difference. Practically the same things happen every day, only to different people, and I don't know them anyway. So what's the odds?"

"Windy—the bedroom philosopher, eh?" Jack laughed.

He put his feet cautiously out of the bed and hastily donned his robe. The room was a refrigerator. He walked over the window, and looked disconsolately out at the dark sky and the overhanging gloom. The wind lashed about outside like a thing alive. The blizzard was still in full force.

"At this rate, we'll be snowed in here all winter," he said in disgust. "I wonder if the phone is working?"

"Who knows?" said Windy, shrugging his shoulders. "Probably not, but why don't you go down and see? Try the one in Max's office."

Jack began dressing rapidly.

"I'm going down anyway," he said. "I want to see if they have Andy's recording of *Headlined in My Heart.*"

"Why?" Windy asked curiously.

"Because I want to hear the way it sounds when the orchestra plays it. There ought to be something there that we should have noticed. And perhaps hearing the way the band plays it under usual conditions will bring it back to me."

"They must have a file of all of Andy's recordings for the past year in the record cabinet. But don't you think you'd better shave first?" suggested Windy. "You never can tell—your girl friend may be there. And anyway, she'll probably drop in later."

Jack rubbed his fingers speculatively over his chin, and examined himself in the mirror. His beard wasn't noticeable yet, but he decided that he wouldn't take a chance on Lee's seeing him that way, so he took out his razor.

"She's not my girl friend, Windy," he said a moment later, emerging momentarily from the bathroom, "but I sure wish she were! What kind of a chance do I stand with a girl like that?"

"Don't be so modest, kid," Windy remarked kindly. "She likes you."

"Do you really think so?" Jack flushed with pleasure, the red of his face contrasting sharply with the white lather. He returned to the bathroom, and hastily finished the job.

Ten minutes later, he was on his way down, wearing his best suit, of a dull blue-green that gave his face a clean, freshly scrubbed look. The corridor was silent, with a somnolent, peaceful quiet, as it would have been at five in the morning almost anywhere else.

Downstairs, the door marked with the request for privacy was still slightly ajar, just as it had been when he first saw it. How like fussy, inefficient Max to leave his office door open all night. He pushed the door open, entered the office, and slammed it shut, but the lock didn't click, and the door slid open again to its original position. So the lock didn't work! Oh, well, it didn't make any difference.

Max's office was small and compactly furnished: with a filing cabinet, a few chairs, a desk—oh, there was the phone. He picked it off its cradle, and held it expectantly to his ear.

He heard nothing. He pressed the cradle a few times in rapid succession, but still a deep and stubborn silence prevailed. No one spoke; no metallic voice uttered the familiar "Numbah, pul-leeze?" So the wires were still un-repaired.

Jack replaced the receiver, yawning lazily, and left the office, promising himself to search it more thoroughly later; also the rooms upstairs, when all the musicians had come down.

He strolled into the dance hall. It was dark and unlit. No daylight had a chance to penetrate there.

What was that? Sounded like music. Was someone playing, at this hour of the morning?

And then, as Jack's eyes grew accustomed to the gloomy darkness, he saw someone sitting at the grand piano on the bandstand—sitting there and playing.

It was Iggy.

Jack walked forward. Iggy was completely absorbed, evidently working on some music—music with strange, unresolved dissonances, with a plaintive haunting strain forcing its way up in the middle register. Jack listened, fascinated, drawn to it as if by a spell. He knew it was original because of the manuscript paper on the piano, on which Iggy was making occasional hasty notes. The sound of Jack's footsteps finally penetrated Iggy's absorption, and he looked up with a vague expression, as if he were coming back from a distance.

"Oh, hello, there!" he called when he recognized Jack. "Up early."

"Yes," answered Jack, walking up on the bandstand to the piano. "I woke up early, so I came down—to listen to some records. How about you?"

"I didn't sleep so well," said Iggy, rubbing his eyes, which were a little bloodshot. "And there's no sense in just tossing around. Only gives me a headache. So I thought I might as well work on an idea I had. This piano is in swell condition—has a wonderful action—and Max, bless him, keeps it tuned in perfect pitch. It's a lot better, of course, than the one inside. And working makes you forget lots of things . . ." Iggy's face once more assumed that moody expression that was almost habitual with him.

"What was that you were playing—when I came in, I mean?" Jack asked hastily to divert him. "It sounded swell!"

"I don't know what it's going to be, yet. Those chords were haunting me, and I thought if I wrote them down and got them out of my system, they'd quit bothering me."

"I wish chords like that would bother me!" Jack said fervently. "Play it for me, please—whatever you have."

"It's still kind of rough—just an idea, really, and it'll take plenty of working out. But what do you think of it—honestly, now?" and Iggy started playing again, improvising over the rough spots. The chords emerged strange and powerful in the bass, and Iggy's long, flexible fingers flashed lightning-like over the keys, scarcely seeming to touch them. Then in the dazzling exhibition of technique came an abrupt change—slow rhythm in the bass, and again that galvanizing melody in the ascendance—as fresh and vital as a spring wind. . . .

"Wait, Iggy!" Jack interrupted excitedly. "Right there, where you switch the tempo, I can *hear* it: four saxes, playing lowdown against a sweet trombone carrying the melody in the middle register, muted trumpets, three of them in harmony, and two clarinets, 'way up, climbing against the ensemble . . . Say, I can *hear* it! Can't you?"

Iggy thought, wrinkling his forehead in his concentration, listening in his mind to Jack's suggested arrangement. A grin of delight spread slowly and ecstatically over his handsome face, transfiguring it with glory.

"That's what I wanted—but exactly! How in the world did you know?" he asked in wonderment.

"Gosh," Jack answered eagerly, "that tune just begs for it. You couldn't do anything else!"

"And right here, where you suggested the clarinets," Iggy continued, his fingers reaching for the keys, "right there, the piano answers back alone, like this—" He demonstrated. ". . . And then the orchestra has its turn—then the whole ensemble, piano and orchestra together . . ."

He kept on as one obsessed, building up to a tremendous climax. Jack felt a choking sensation. Such beauty was almost unbearable.

"What I wouldn't give to orchestrate that!" he breathed wistfully. "It simply orchestrates itself."

"Say, would you?" Iggy asked eagerly. "I can arrange, of course, but you seem to hear what I want better than I can."

"Orchestration is just a knack, a technique—but writing like yours is genius," Jack said simply.

Iggy flushed, and smiled shyly. "Oh, I'm not that good," he said. "Genius is a word that's always being used much too loosely as a synonym for talent. But—well, it's gratifying to hear another musician so enthusiastic about my stuff. I'd like to call this thing *Swing Concerto*. You know, make it in strict concerto form for piano and orchestra, using the modern jazz idiom—"

He interrupted himself suddenly, and laughed bitterly, mocking his own enthusiasm.

"Listen to me, will you? Next thing you know, I'll be putting in a reservation for Carnegie Hall for my first performance—swelled head and all!"

"Don't be so damned modest!" said Jack impatiently. "Diffidence has no place in this business. People usually take you at your own face value, so if you keep saying you're good, after a while they'll begin to believe you, especially when a guy has something on the ball, as you have. If you know you're good, why be afraid to think seriously of furthering yourself? And Carnegie isn't as far out of your reach as you seem to think. Look at the swing concerts they've had there recently, and boogie-woogie, too, no less! So why can't you perform a serious work there? Just because it's in a new idiom doesn't mean it's any the less serious."

"Thanks for the pep talk, Coach," Iggy laughed. "Now I'll go in and tear the hell out of those highbrows. But seriously, I feel very strongly about this subject of American music. Of course, the longhairs aren't as prejudiced as they used to be, thanks to Gershwin, but there are still plenty of people with their noses stuck so high up in the air that they can't see what's under them. They don't realize how much wonderful material there is right here."

"You said it!" Jack agreed enthusiastically. "There's a lot more to it than just rhythm to dance to, or a chance for a lot of instruments to do a little plain and fancy improvising, with the drum playing the melody!

"And talking about dances, you've heard how the waltz and even the gavotte and minuet were at one time considered short cuts to immorality. But look what the big figures in classical music—the three B's—did with them. It's comparable in our time to Beethoven writing a symphony with a boogie-woogie or lindy-hop movement in place of the allegro."

"I never thought of that," said Iggy.

"And don't be a nit-wit!" Jack continued forcefully. "That wasn't just empty talk about your preparing that thing for a concert. Go ahead with the concerto—finish it! And I think I can orchestrate it to your taste. I—er—did that arrangement of *Rockin' Chair Variations* that Louie Carter recorded, and then used on his tour."

"No kidding!" Iggy's amazement was gratifying. He was very evidently impressed, even more than Windy had been.

"You're O.K., Red! Say, let's shake on that collaboration, then. We're going to do big things together."

They shook hands very solemnly. Then Iggy became dejected.

"Ha!" he exclaimed. "Here we are, shooting off our mouths about the wonderful things that we're going to do. Wait till the police come and the band gets it in the neck! Who knows what's ahead of us!"

"Oh, don't worry about it till it happens," said Jack, trying hard to be optimistic. But he too was recalled to their present problems that seemed so impossible of a satisfactory solution.

What a mess they were all in! And here he was, committed to working with Iggy, who might conceivably be a murderer—anything was possible! Again his suspicions started revolving in that endless, weary cycle, round and round, covering the same ground. Who could have done it, and why?

Iggy's fit of composing had worn itself out. He started rising from the piano stool.

"I'll work on that thing some more later—if I ever get in the mood again," he said pessimistically.

"Wait a minute," said Jack, detaining him, "Do me a favor, huh?"

"Sure. What is it?"

"Just run over the chorus of *Headlined in My Heart,* please—I mean the part you have in the orchestration."

Iggy looked at him with an inscrutable expression in his dark eyes. He was about to say something; then, evidently changing his mind, he sat down again, and played. His hands moved among the keys indifferently, with a curious sort of detachment. Jack watched him furtively, noting his elbows, the way he sat.

That was the position he had been in when— But could he have played and turned around at the same time? Wouldn't his left elbow have been twisted unnaturally?

Jack looked toward the center of the bandstand, the spot the spotlight would enclose. It was almost inconceivable that Andy would have twisted his body so much that his back would have become a target from this angle.

But his job wasn't to discover whether it was probable that Iggy had shot him, but whether it was possible.

Jack thought not.

Iggy came to the end of the song, and banged out the last note in the bass with his left index finger, a cynical expression on his face. In all probability, he knew exactly why Jack had asked him to play his piano part of the song.

"Gosh!" exclaimed Jack hastily, to cover up. "I'm crazy about those chords you used, with the melody following them so simply. It has so much color to it."

"Talking about harmony," Iggy said, his face lighting up again, as he rose from the piano, "have you heard that new Duke Ellington tune yet? The one that came out last week?"

"No, I haven't. What's it like?"

"Let's go in the lounge, and you can hear it," said Iggy, leading the way. "I have the recording there. Just couldn't resist buying it. Talk about not being a prophet in your own country—in England, Duke Ellington is considered one of the finest composers in the small form that America has produced so far. But is he properly appreciated here? Not on your life!"

He went on in the same vein, speaking with heartfelt enthusiasm, and as he spoke, Jack watched his gaunt, handsome face, trying to reconcile this eager-faced boy with the murder suspect he might become when the police finally arrived. It was unthinkable, uncharacteristic. Iggy obviously worked out his emotional stress in music. That was his outlet, his safety valve. He was wise enough to work out his heartache. Or so it seemed. . . .

Iggy was still deep in a technical discussion of Ellington and his place in modern music when they opened the door to the lounge.

". . . Take *Hot and Bothered,* for instance. His record-ing of that is pretty close to perfection. And what's wrong with his *Creole Fantasy? . . .*"

He stopped as they entered the room.

Someone was sitting in an armchair against the farthest wall.

"Why, it's Tony!" Iggy said in surprise. "Hey, you early bird! It's not even ten. Have you been here all night?"

Tony didn't answer.

"Tony?" Iggy said again, uncertainly.

They came closer.

Tony sat there, looking at them with a surprised, un-comprehending stare. Jack's scalp prickled unaccountably.

And then they saw it—that strange, red-rimmed little hole, right between the eyes. . . .

"God in heaven!" exclaimed Iggy with a smothered gasp. "He's dead. . . . M-murdered, too!"

# 11

Iggy sat down limply on the nearest chair, his legs folding under him as though they could no longer hold him up. Jack stood there silently, staring at the scene before him, trying to take it all in.

All sorts of vague, half formulated thoughts and impressions rushed through his mind. Tony still had his tux on. . . . The lights were on. . . . And there was another chair drawn up to Tony's. . . . Someone had been there with him, then, talking to him perhaps. . . . There had been little bleeding. . . . Probably he had been killed instantly, like Andy. . . . Taken by surprise, too, because there was no sign whatever of a struggle. . . . No gun anywhere around, so it was murder, definitely . . .

Jack leaned over the body, and touched the wrist. The flesh felt cold and clammy. Then his eye fell on a card lying near the chair on the floor. He picked it up, holding it by the edges. It was an ordinary identification card, and bore Tony's name, address, and telephone number. But why was it on the floor? It was the sort of thing a man kept in his wallet . . . His wallet . . . !

Jack made a sudden decision. This wasn't exactly according to Hoyle, but he was going to search Tony anyway. He emptied Tony's pockets. In an outside jacket pocket he found Tony's wallet. This contained more of those cards, some money, a driving license, his union card, and a picture of a girl.

Why was that card on the floor? Had Tony taken out his wallet to remove something, so that the card had fallen out accidentally? But wait a minute—the wallet had been in his jacket pocket where a man would ordinarily keep cigarettes. And there had been a pack in with the wallet. But why would Tony put his wallet in that pocket?

It should have been in his inside pocket. Definitely not where it was now. Didn't that indicate that someone had searched him after he was dead? That someone had removed the wallet, and then had put it back in the most accessible place? It would have been awkward to shift the dead man around too much. And had that person killed Tony for something the wallet contained? If so, that person had obtained it, because nothing illuminating in the slightest remained in that wallet.

Shouldn't there have been a cancelled check?

The room was still in disorder. It hadn't been cleaned since the previous night. The ash trays were still filled to overflowing, the room was dusty and, unaired, and the whiskey glasses dirty and sticky.

Jack searched half-heartedly for a gun, under the seat cushions, behind the tables, in the drawers. He didn't expect to find one.

Had the same person killed both Tony and Andy?

Iggy had been there on the bandstand alone this morning. He had been playing there, while inside, Tony sat dead . . .

Iggy was white. He stared at Tony as if his eyes were unable to focus properly.

"Did the same one kill both of them?" he asked in a trembling voice, suddenly voicing Jack's thoughts.

"I think that's the only logical conclusion," Jack answered absent-mindedly, still looking about the room.

"Logical!" Iggy exclaimed passionately. "What's logical about this—this—! It isn't logical . . . it's horrible! To think we were out there gabbing about music, and Tony was in here dead! I was playing *Headlined in My Heart* and Tony was in here dead! That song—it's a jinx, I tell you—a jinx! It hasn't done anyone any good, ever since I wrote it! Brought me hard luck; then Andy died singing it; and now—now Tony— Why the hell did I ever write the damn thing?" he concluded bitterly.

"Come now, Iggy, don't you think you're being a little far-fetched?" Jack asked, trying to reassure the pianist. "It had nothing whatever to do with the song, and you'd be childishly superstitious if you really believed it did. Someone here hated Andy, and killed him. The same goes for Tony—" Jack paused reflectively, then continued more slowly—"only I have an idea that Tony was probably killed because he knew too much. . . ."

"Well, how do you know that it was the same person?" Iggy persisted, the color returning gradually to his face.

"Someone had a gun," Jack answered, thinking his way carefully. "It would be too much of a coincidence to suppose that *two* people had guns, and each had a murderous intention toward a different person. It's possible, of course, but not probable—against the laws of chance; and in life it's the probable thing that usually happens."

"But what was Tony doing here, and still dressed, too?" Iggy asked with an air of bewilderment. "We all went up to bed. I saw him go into his room with Jimmy."

"Yes, he did," Jack informed him. "I know he was in his room at least for a while last night, because Windy and I both heard him talking through the bathroom door. So that means that he came down here after that, perhaps to look for something, or to talk to someone. But the fact that he's still wearing his tux, and that the lights are still on, proves that this must have happened last night."

"I wish that storm would stop acting like something from *East Lynne* so we could get the police," Iggy said, looking unhappily out of the window. "I don't like this at all. By the way, are the phones still out of order?"

"Yes," answered Jack. "I tried the one in Max's office just before I saw you."

"Well, then, I guess I'd better go call the others. You can wait here and watch—watch Tony."

"Wait, Iggy," Jack said thoughtfully. "Tony doesn't exactly need watching any longer. We'll go up and call each fellow in turn, tell them what happened, and observe their faces to see how they take it. How about it—want to help me out?"

"Whatever you say," answered Iggy, but a shadow of distaste for the job flitted across his face. "Only—I don't think any of the boys did it. It wouldn't make sense . . . ."

"You have to face the fact that someone here is dangerous," said Jack practically as they walked out. "It's simply got to be one of them, unless Orson Welles has turned his Martians loose again. And incidentally, Iggy," he continued as they walked up the stairs, "what were you doing last night?"

Iggy's eyes narrowed. Then he smiled ruefully.

"I see—just one of the suspects," he said. "So I need an alibi. Well, let's see now . . . Buddy and I went right to bed, but I didn't sleep so well."

"Buddy is your roommate, then?" Jack interrupted him.

"Yeah. So as I was saying, I didn't sleep so well, and I woke up early. 'Bout eight, I guess it was. I got restless just lying in bed, so I dressed, and went down to do some work, just as I told you before. That's all I know, honestly."

"What about Buddy? Was he awake when you left your room this morning?"

"No. He was still sleeping."

"And when you came down, you didn't go into the lounge at all?"

"No," asserted Iggy. "I sat myself right down at the piano on the bandstand. I told you that one was much better than the one in the lounge. And I brought manuscript paper with me—I keep some in my room, I thought the lounge was empty. It usually is, till about twelve."

"Perhaps we'll be able to get some clues now," said Jack as they paused outside the first bedroom door in the corridor. "It stands to reason that it will be twice as hard for the killer to get away with two crimes without leaving some trace."

He turned the knob.

"That's Andy's room!" exclaimed Iggy, detaining him. "Why do you want to go in there?"

"It won't hurt to give the place the once-over, just to see if anything's been touched."

The sheeted figure on the bed looked unreal and ghostly in the commonplace surroundings. Jack walked in softly, and noticed that everything was exactly as it had been when they had brought Andy up.

"Come on!" urged Iggy. "Let's get out of here. You can't ask him any questions."

"Well, we'll soon have company for him—to occupy that empty bed," Jack remarked with grim humor as they left.

"Do you know," he continued as they paused before the next door, "it occurs to me that Ray slept alone last night, so he's the one person that can't possibly have an alibi for the time after we went to bed."

"Oh, no!" Iggy whispered, aghast. "Ray wouldn't have done it. Why should he? He never quarreled particularly with Tony, or, for that matter, with Andy either. He's the kind of guy that doesn't say much. Just minds his own business."

"Now listen to me, Iggy. You've got to stop thinking of these people as your friends and face facts. One of them is dangerous enough to have killed two people. The mind of a murderer is warped. He's insane. So don't have any compunctions about trying to discover who this maniac is—friend or no friend."

Iggy shook his head stubbornly. "I can't imagine who of us could have—could have done anything so coldblooded . . ."

Jack opened the next door softly. Only one bed in the room was occupied. The other was still made up neatly, bedspread and all. Everything was orderly and neat, the clothes folded away, and hung up properly. The impersonal room had overnight taken on Ray's precise personality.

There was a mound in the occupied bed, a figure covered completely by the bedclothes. For a moment, Jack had the feeling that this room was also full of death, like the one they had just left. He shook the sensation off.

"Ray's still sleeping," Iggy whispered. "I hope he isn't sore because we barged in like this without knocking. He's such a stickler for little details."

"What are we supposed to do—send in a butler with our calling cards?" Jack asked sardonically as he approached the bed. "Or maybe we should write to Emily Post and ask her about the proper procedure for notifying someone of a recently occurred violent death?"

Jack turned the bedclothes down, revealing Ray's face. His eyes were closed, and he appeared to be deep in a peaceful, conscience-clear slumber. His face looked a little strange, naked somehow, until Jack realized that he was seeing the saxophonist for the first time without his glasses.

Ray suddenly opened his eyes. He sat up, peering nearsightedly at Jack.

"What's the matter?" he yawned when he recognized them. "Andy want a rehearsal?"

He reached for the glasses in their case on the table beside the bed. Then all at once he remembered, and eyed them suspiciously. "What's wrong?" he repeated, an expression of alertness on his face.

"Tony has been murdered—downstairs in the lounge!" Iggy blurted out.

"Wha-at?" Ray looked first incredulous, then bewildered. Jack watched him closely, trying to discover whether his surprise was assumed or genuine. Someone was going to be putting on an act when notified. As far as he could tell, Ray really was surprised.

Ray thought a moment, then asked calmly:

"Have you thought that Tony might have been the one who killed Andy, and then have decided to commit suicide?"

"No," Jack said decisively. "That's absolutely out! He was shot, and there was no gun around. Better get dressed as soon as you can and come down. We're going to wake the others, and tell them to come down too, so we can thrash it out."

"Right!" And Ray began dressing quickly, wasting no time in futile protestations or questions. Or didn't Ray have to ask questions? Did he know the answers?

"The next room's mine," said Iggy, opening the door.

Buddy was sleeping flat on his back, snoring lightly. He was uncovered, the bedclothes having slid over the edge of the bed to the floor. The striped scarlet and white pajamas made him resemble a stick of peppermint candy. His mouth was slightly open, and with his tousled hair, he looked about twelve.

Iggy shook his shoulder lightly as if loath to disturb him.

"Get up, kid," he said gently.

Buddy opened one eye, then shut it again. "Scram!" he said thickly.

"Come on, Buddy," Iggy insisted. "Wake up!"

Buddy's eyes remained shut, and his face retained its placid expression. Iggy pulled the pillow roughly from under his head.

Buddy opened his eyes, and sat up quickly with an injured expression.

"Oh, you wanna play! Why didn't you say so?" And he leaned over, grabbing the pillow from Iggy's bed. Iggy stopped him before he could throw it.

"Quit the clowning, Buddy. Something terrible has happened!"

Buddy eyed them quizzically. "Now don't tell me that Andy has come back to life!"

"Tony has been murdered!" Jack said, his eyes never leaving the young first trumpeter's face.

Buddy looked baffled. Then he laughed.

"You know," he said conversationally, "I don't think my hearing's been so good lately. Just now, it sounded to me as if you said that Tony had been murdered." He glanced at Iggy.

"It's true," Iggy said. "We just found him dead in the lounge."

"Honest? This isn't just a gag?" Buddy's ordinarily pale skin whitened even more. "Was—was Tony shot, too?"

They nodded assent.

Buddy's thin face became awed. He pushed the unruly mop of dark hair off his forehead with a thoughtful air. Then his face brightened suddenly, and his eyebrows went up in a pixie fashion.

"Say! Maybe someone is just trying to pare the band down to a trio, eh? Small combinations are becoming the vogue now."

"Get dressed, Buddy," Jack advised him, solemnly refusing to laugh. "And make it snappy! Also, better go easy on the wisecracks. Two murders aren't in the least bit funny."

Buddy's face took on a little-boy look of contrition. He got out of bed, saying: "O.K., I'll be right down."

"Don't be hard on him," said Iggy, after they left. "He doesn't mean any harm when he cuts up. You see, he came from an orphanage, and—well, he's always afraid of being kicked around, so he wisecracks just to make believe he doesn't care about anything. He's really a decent kid underneath it all."

Jack took this plea on Buddy's behalf with reservations. They were loyal to each other, these two. Would one cover up something serious to save the other?

"This is Si and Frankie's room," said Iggy as he opened the next door. They walked in softly.

Si was still sleeping, just as he had been when they had looked in on him the night before. He was still in his tux, and snoring heavily.

Frankie had been sleeping when they entered, but the click of the door as it closed aroused him. The drummer looked wide-eyed at them, his Adam's apple working convulsively in his scrawny neck.

"What's wrong?" he asked quickly.

"Tony is dead!" Jack announced. "You'd better get dressed and come downstairs as quickly as possible."

Fear clouded Frankie's eyes.

"What do you mean—dead?"

"Murdered!" Jack said succinctly.

Frankie's bony face seemed to shrink before their eyes. He swallowed convulsively.

"This place—it's a madhouse!" he mumbled as he reached for his pants.

"Scared, Frankie?" Iggy asked softly.

"Yes, I am!" came the belligerent answer. "And I don't care who knows it! There's a maniac loose in this joint, and here we are, cooped up—no police, no phone—and we can't get out! Damn! Why wasn't I something nice and respectable—like a union plumber? If I ever get out of here alive, I'll never take another job unless it's right under the Wrigley sign on Times Square!" His hands shook as he dressed, and he looked badly frightened. They watched him, and their silent scrutiny maddened him.

"Maybe you think I did it," he rasped. "Well, I didn't! I didn't!"

Methinks the drummer doth protest too much, thought Jack. Why was Frankie so terrified? Was it just a bad attack of nerves? Too much drinking, too much smoking . . . Perhaps he had been one of Tony's customers.

Jack's eye fell on Si, who was still snoring placidly.

"Was Si still sleeping when you came up last night, Frankie?" he asked.

"Yeah. He snored like the devil—kept me awake practically the whole night. You'll never wake him up until he's slept his jag off. I know him by now."

Iggy shook the sleeping guitarist. Then Jack tried to arouse him, but they discovered that Frankie was right. Si continued snoring undisturbed.

"Save your strength," advised Frankie. "I'm telling you he won't come out of it until he's good and ready."

"Oh, Frankie," Iggy said kindly, "don't you think you'd better take your pajamas off before you try putting your pants on?"

"Cripes!" muttered Frankie, looking down. "So that's what the matter is!"

They walked out, leaving him mumbling to himself about never leaving Broadway and Forty-Second again.

"Has that guy got it bad!" Iggy exclaimed. "Do you think he—"

"I don't know. It does seem to me, though, that he's too scared to be the murderer. Unless, of course, he's just putting on an act. You know him better than I do, Iggy. What do you think?"

"I guess you're right. He is always like that—afraid of his own shadow. He won't go in a dark corner by himself."

"His mother must have been frightened by Boris Karloff," laughed Jack. "Still, although I hate to keep repeating this, we've got to suspect everyone. You'd better suspect me, and just to keep the records straight, I'll suspect you."

Iggy gave him an odd, sidelong glance. "You don't really suspect me, do you? Otherwise you wouldn't be trying to discover who did do it, and you wouldn't let me come with you now."

"Of course I think you did it," Jack grinned. "I'm taking you along with me so that I can keep an eye on you, and I'm trying to pin it on someone else, because you couldn't finish your concerto in jail."

"Well, anyway, I could do some boogie-woogie variations on the *Prisoner's Song* there," Iggy answered, his eyes twinkling. They both laughed.

"Here we are at my door," said Jack. "Windy's in here by himself."

"What would he know about it?" asked Iggy. "He never even saw the boys here before tonight. And if our beloved leader had known him from somewhere else, Andy would have made a characteristic nasty remark about it soon enough."

"I know. But we may as well tell him about it. He may have some helpful ideas." Windy'd think of Jimmy, too, he finished to himself.

Windy was still reading the paper. He looked up as they entered, and grinned with glee.

"Look at this article, will ya?" he chortled. "'Is Swing On Its Way Out?' Gosh, those guys ought to save the paper it's written on. As far as those sob sisters are concerned, it's been on the way out ever since it came in. Why don't they write an article on 'Is Sex Here To Stay?' while they're at it?"

"Windy," Jack interrupted him, "Tony is dead."

Windy looked up quickly from the offending article. "Dead! What's up?"

"He was murdered—just like Andy."

Windy glanced silently toward the bathroom door. His eyes met Jack's.

"In his room?" he asked laconically.

"No. He was shot in the lounge."

"Mm." Windy wrinkled his high forehead. "Do you think—" and he nodded toward Jimmy's room.

"Maybe," Jack said, shrugging his shoulders. "We haven't told him yet. Anyway, he has an awful lot of explaining to do."

Iggy listened bewildered to their esoteric exchange.

"You two seem to know something about someone," he broke in. "Mind letting me in on it?"

"Downstairs," Jack promised him.

"I'll get dressed," Windy said. He sighed patiently. "Now we have to go over the same routine, huh? Boy, are we in a rut!"

"Right!" Jack nodded. "See you in the lounge. We're going to round up the last of the bunch now."

Outside, they paused in front of the last occupied room: Jimmy's—and Tony's.

Jimmy was lying in bed, awake, when they entered. He paled, then flushed, and Jack could see tiny beads of sweat glistening on his upper lip. The heavy shadows under his eyes testified to a sleepless night.

When he saw them, Jimmy sat up in bed and wet his lips with his tongue.

"What happened?" he asked hoarsely.

Jack touched Iggy's arm, restraining him from speaking. He asked: "What makes you think something has happened?"

Jimmy stared at him without replying.

"Where's Tony?" Jack asked casually. The other bed hadn't been slept in at all.

Jimmy shook his head, but as Jack waited implacably for an answer, he gulped audibly, and finally said:

"He—he said he wanted to sleep by himself tonight. Maybe I snore, or—or something. . . ." His voice faded away unconvincingly. Then he continued: "He must be in one of the other rooms, or—oh, how the hell should I know where he is?"

Jack walked over to the chair beside Tony's bed. There was a clean pair of pajamas folded on it, and over the back, a dressing gown had been thrown.

"He didn't take any pajamas with him, then?"

"How should I know?" Jimmy repeated belligerently. "What am I—his nurse, or his valet?" And he lay down again, covering himself with the bedclothes.

Jack saw the ashtray on the table beside the bed, and went over to examine it more closely. It contained cigarette butts—lots of them—and cigarette ashes. Also the ashes of something else—bits of charred paper. Something had been burned there recently, and it didn't take too much thinking to deduce what that paper had been.

"What are you looking for?" Jimmy asked in a frightened voice, his eyes dilating.

"You know as well as I do," Jack answered ominously. "Maybe better. Tony is downstairs—dead!"

Jimmy's face turned a peculiar yellow shade.

"D-dead!" he repeated. "Who—"

"That's just what we're trying to find out."

"Why don't you look for the gun?" Jimmy asked weakly. "Someone must have a gun to do all this shooting."

"No doubt!" agreed Jack with irony, as he and Iggy exchanged meaningful glances. "But who told you that Tony was shot?"

Jimmy blanched.

"He was, though, wasn't he? Andy was shot, so Tony must have been, too. What are you trying to do—trap me?"

"You're doing all right by yourself," Iggy interrupted. "Get dressed and come downstairs. And you'd better be thinking up a good story."

Jimmy's eyes did not meet his. He reached for his robe, his round young face set in a sullen mold.

"I'll be right down," he muttered.

Iggy paused outside in the corridor, a worried look on his face.

"Sounds as if he knows something, doesn't he? I suppose he's the one you and Windy were talking about before. You think he's guilty, don't you?"

Jack rubbed his chin speculatively.

"Can't tell yet. But he certainly knows something. Otherwise, why should he be so frightened? He's not like Frankie. And I can tell you this: Jimmy had excellent motives for both murders."

# 12

"Well!" thought Jack, a short time later, when they had all gathered once more in the lounge, "so history repeats itself—or I should say, Mystery repeats itself. Oh, damn, now Buddy's got me doing it too."

Most of the boys were unshaven, dressed hastily in the first thing that had been around—some in slacks and sweaters, and Frankie had put on his tux again. They looked disreputable, and frightened or disturbed to various degrees.

Jimmy, his face pale and pinched-looking, was sitting by himself, smoking incessantly. He kept lighting a cigarette, letting it burn halfway through, then extinguishing it nervously and lighting another, chain style. The pile of half smoked butts in the ash tray beside him was mountainous. If ever there was a picture of a guilty person—

Suddenly the silence seemed to become too much for Jimmy to bear.

"Well, what are you waiting for?" he asked Jack, and his voice contained hysterical overtones. "Why don't you begin asking your damned questions?"

So there was something on his chest—something he was afraid to tell, and afraid not to. He didn't appear to have the coolness and nerve which would have been necessary to carry Andy's murder off successfully.

"Windy," Jack said, ignoring Jimmy's outburst completely, "go into the kitchen, please, and get one of the waiters to bring us some breakfast—although I understand it's customary for you boys to eat in the dining room under ordinary circumstances. So if you'd rather eat there—"

"Who wants chow anyway?" Jimmy asked irritably.

"Me!" Buddy spoke up. "The day I can't eat—well, then I'll probably have become one of our Mr. X's clients."

"Unless," said Frankie, looking at him suspiciously, *"you're* Mr. X!"

"How you do go on, Mr. Jannings!" Buddy simpered. "Bet you say that to all the boys!"

"I think we had better eat here," suggested Ray. "Max's hotel guests will probably look at us as if we were the plague, with those kids telling tales."

"O.K.," Windy said agreeably. "I'll go."

"And, Windy," added Jack, "if Max is there, don't tell him about Tony. Just ask him to come in here as soon as possible. Tell him I have something to ask him."

No one spoke for a time after Windy left. Jimmy kept staring at the chair in which they had discovered Tony. Frankie watched him covertly, then suddenly shifted his chair nervously and rasped in his fog-horn voice:

"Stop staring at that chair, will you? What do you see there anyhow?"

Jimmy started, then looked defiantly at the others.

"I d-didn't know I was looking at it. I—er—was thinking about something else," he stammered. Ray came over and examined the chair, peering closely at the polished arms.

"Look!" he exclaimed. "There are fingerprints all over the chair. Also on the table right nearby. That should tell the experts a thing or two."

"Sure!" jeered Buddy. "It'll tell them that we've all been in this room, and at one time or another touched it, legitimately. We all belong here, remember? I know," he continued brightly, "let's go out and look for the gun again!"

Not while Jack had anything to say about it, they weren't! The time to have looked for the gun, to have searched them all, would have been right after Andy had been killed, when they were all on the platform, and when no one had had an opportunity to dispose of the weapon. But he hadn't thought of it then. And even if he had, they'd probably have objected to being searched. As Ray had said, he—Jack—had no real authority.

He was saved the necessity of negating Buddy's proposal by the entrance of two waiters with trays of food. They were followed by Max and Windy.

Max looked weary and disgruntled.

"G'morning, fellers," he muttered. "Windy said you wanted to see me, Jack."

"How's the hotel business?" Jack asked.

"You have to call me in to ask me that, yet? Don't ask! Those lousy kids are making it hot for me—the girls hollering they wanna go home, and the boys sticking their noses in everything. They keep asking my guests where they were on the night of June the Sixteenth. They're crazy, so help me! What kind of a holiday is June the Sixteenth, anyway? If I have one guest when this thing is over, I'll be lucky! They're all old maids and bachelors who like my place because it's quiet. Quiet! Ha! This morning I found one of the kids in the kitchen, pestering my cook. He's a Swede, and doesn't understand much English, and that kid was driving him wild. Now my cook is threatening to quit. So I gave the kid a little of what was in my heart—you know, tried to scare him a little by telling him that if he didn't behave he'd go to jail. And do you know what? That little snotnose starts yapping about his constitutional rights! What about *my* constitutional rights, I wanna know! Believe me, what's happening to me shouldn't happen to a dog!"

Max's expression was so woebegone that Jack wanted to laugh. A snicker did escape involuntarily, so he turned around hastily and began collecting some breakfast for himself.

Frankie was looking with great disgust at Buddy, who was helping himself methodically to a lot of everything: fruit juice, cereal, mounds of toast, hot and buttered, scrambled eggs, and coffee. The others were following suit, although not quite so enthusiastically. Jimmy, however, sat where he was, smoking stubbornly, avoiding the sight of the food.

Max watched the wholesale demolition of the breakfast supplies, then said hastily: "I had my breakfast already, but the coffee smells good. Guess I'll have another cup." Whereupon he heaped a platter with most of the remaining food, and set to with the others, hungrily wolfing the contents of his plate.

It was a shame to spoil the little man's appetite, thought Jack as he dug into his own scrambled eggs, but he might as well get it over with.

"Oh, Max," he said casually, taking another bite out of his toast, "where were you last night after you left here?"

"When do you mean?" Max looked puzzled.

"Did you go right to bed as soon as you left here?"

"Nah! Who could sleep? Let's see. First I went to Kitty's room with Lee, who slept with her last night. So at the same time, I stopped in to see how Kitty was feeling. She was awake when we came in, and when she saw me, she started carrying on again about Andy. So Lee made me leave. I didn't feel like going to bed yet, so I went to my office—the one in the hotel. Cohen, my hotel manager, was there, checking over the accounts. He's a jewel, I tell you, a jewel!" Max's face glowed with pleasure at the thought of his treasure, Cohen.

"He studied Hotel Management at Cornell," Max continued. "He's one of these real efficiency experts. Sometimes I think he cares more about the hotel than I do, and he certainly saves me money, so I let him have complete charge of the hotel, and I take care of the Casino. Let me tell you, that guy works for that place night and day. Imagine, it's nearly twelve o'clock last night, and I find him still checking over the accounts, looking where he can save. A penny here, a penny there—like Cohen says—it all mounts up." Max concluded his glowing eulogy of Cohen, and sat there beaming his pleasure.

Jack listened to this rambling testimonial with great patience.

"How long did you stay there?" he asked finally, bringing him back to the subject.

"Oh, we talked till about four in the morning. He has insomnia too, and we were telling each other our troubles. He's kind of worried about how this publicity will affect the hotel's reputation." Max's face resumed its familiar harassed expression. "And those lousy kids! If they'd only leave the guests alone—"

"Look, Max," said Jack, gently but firmly putting a halt to this vague flow of words, "am I to understand that this Cohen will testify that you were with him from the time you left Kitty until four o'clock this morning?"

"Sure," Max asserted. "But why does he have to testify about that time? Andy was killed early. Say, what are all those questions for?"

"You see, Max—while you were talking to your friend Cohen, someone murdered Tony!"

Max wrinkled his frizzled gray eyebrows uncomprehendingly. Suddenly he looked wildly about him as if expecting Tony's body to pop out at him.

"Wh-where is he?"

"We found him dead here in the lounge this morning. In that chair, as a matter of fact. We took him upstairs before you came in."

Max put his cup down, his hands shaking so that the coffee slopped over into the saucer. The stubby fingers of his right hand clutched the cup handle so tightly that the joints resembled cocktail sausages.

He looked down blankly at his food, then uttered a small whimpering sound. "This place—it's a lunatic asylum! Wh-what's going on here? Who killed Tony?"

"I know," Buddy volunteered. "Cohen killed Andy and Tony to keep the hotel from getting a bad name."

"Cohen didn't kill anyone!" Max screamed, outraged at this heresy. "You think he's—he's a good-for-nothing like you, you crazy musician, you!"

"Buddy is only joking," Jack interposed, trying to calm him down. "You and Cohen give each other fairly good alibis, so take it easy, eh?"

"Him and his jokes!" Max subsided slowly, giving Buddy a black look.

Just then the door opened, and Lee entered. She was wearing a black wool skirt and a fuzzy scarlet sweater, with a jaunty scarlet bow catching her curls in back. She herself looked far from jaunty, however—more as if she had spent a sleepless night. There were mauve shadows under her eyes.

"Hi, boys!" she greeted them, smiling tiredly at the room in general. "Did any ghosts walk last night?"

At the solemn silence that met her flippant greeting, her expression became more serious, and questioning.

"Lee," Jack said without preliminaries, "after Max deposited you at Kitty's room, did you leave it at all?"

"No, of course not. Why?"

"You're sure?" Jack insisted. "You went right to sleep?"

"Well, I didn't exactly sleep. What's been happening hasn't exactly had soporific effects. Besides, Kitty just wouldn't get to sleep again. She kept talking me deaf, dumb, and blind about Andy—how wonderful he was, how kind, how good-natured, and how unselfish!" Lee smiled a crooked, bitter smile. "At least it was such a new angle on Andy that it wasn't boring. I just lay there and listened in amazement."

"About what time did you fall asleep? Do you know?"

"'Long about three-thirty, I guess it was. I made Kitty take another aspirin, and she finally dozed off. So I followed suit. She's still sleeping now."

"In other words, you and Kitty were together from the time you left the lounge, approximately—right?"

"You sound as though you were trying to establish an alibi for me," she said, a terrified expression appearing on her face. "What's wrong? Tell me! Has something happened?" She looked about the room, moving carefully from face to face, checking up on the members of the group.

"Si is missing! Si, and—and Tony! It's Tony, isn't it?"

"Yes, Lee," Jack answered her. "Tony is dead, too. He was murdered sometime between the time we went to bed and this morning. Probably soon after we got to bed, I should say from the condition of the body."

Lee sat down, stunned and wordless.

Iggy arose tensely. "If I have to hear once more that Tony is dead," he said, "I'll—I'll do something desperate!"

"Let's write out a note for Si, then," suggested Buddy. "Tell him all about it."

"Si doesn't even know that Andy is dead yet," Ray said.

"I'm sure that he'll take the bad news like a little man! I know what—" And that impish expression flashed across Buddy's face. "When he comes down, we'll say they're both still sleeping, and send Si up to wake them. Oh, boy! Can you imagine his face when he sees them! After that, he'll jump on the water wagon so fast he'll make Jesse Owens look like Stepin Fetchit!"

"You and your bright ideas!" Frankie exclaimed, grimacing with disgust. "This ain't just an excuse for you to exercise your alleged sense of humor. It's murder!"

"Well," Jack said, mentally girding up his loins again, "who knows anything? Anyone hear the shot?"

His question was met with blank stares.

"Come now," persisted Jack, pulling at a lock of his red hair with a baffled feeling of frustration. "Didn't anyone hear the sound of a shot last night?"

"Not through these walls," Max finally contributed. "They're too solid. You can't hear anything through this ceiling."

"Well, then," Jack tried another tack, "if anyone knows anything—anything at all—I think it would be wise for that person to say so now. It's dangerous not to!"

He waited, but no one spoke.

"You see," he continued, "Max and Lee both seem to have alibis, as far as I can see. There are seven of the band left. Si is out. He couldn't possibly have killed Andy, and Frankie has given him an alibi for Tony's death. That leaves six. And among these six is a two-time killer—someone who is desperate!"

# 13

"Who has an alibi?" Jack asked.

"The sixty-four dollar question, boys!" Buddy mocked. "The question no one can answer. Who has an alibi? Hm!"

"How about yours, Jack?" Ray asked gently. "You're simply one of the boys now, you know."

"I can vouch for Jack," Windy spoke up. "We came up together, went to sleep, and since I'm a light sleeper, I'm positive he'd've wakened me if he had left the bedroom. Besides, this is the first time either Jack or I have met any of you, and that, of course, goes for Tony and Andy as well. So neither of us has a motive."

"Thanks, Windy," Jack said lightly. "That seems to take care of us for a while. Now, who else?"

"Iggy and I talked half the night," Buddy said. "I can swear that we didn't leave each other's sight from the time we came up till this morning."

"That's right," Iggy verified. "I guess Buddy and I alibi each other."

"Very definite, isn't he?" Ray said. "Those two are like *Cavalleria Rusticana* and *Pagliacci*—inseparable. They'd swear black is white for each other."

"Look, wise guy," Buddy exploded angrily, *"you* can't afford to be sceptical! You were completely alone all of last night. So you have some heavy explaining to do."

"So I have no alibi." Ray apparently was completely undisturbed. "So what? After all," he continued, glancing at Iggy, "I didn't have a fist fight with Tony the night before he was killed."

"There isn't much you can swear to, Buddy," Jack added kindly, "except that you and Iggy went to bed at the same time. You didn't wake up when he left your room early this morning, did you?"

"No, I didn't," Buddy admitted defiantly, his pointed chin set stubbornly. "But I can swear that we both fell asleep pretty late—maybe three, maybe four in the morning." And he glared about the room with a challenging air.

"Don't be so vehement in my defense, Buddy," Iggy said with an indulgent smile. "After all, I'm not guilty, so you needn't work so hard preparing an alibi for me."

Buddy sat back with a shamefaced expression.

Jack turned his attention to Ray. "Did you go right to bed last night?"

"Yes, I did. I slept very soundly, and didn't awaken until you came into my room this morning."

"And how about you, Frankie?" Jack continued. "Si isn't in a position to give you much of an alibi."

"Guess he can't," admitted the drummer. "Not unless he identifies me among those pink elephants he probably saw marching around all night."

"I'll take the pink elephants any time," Buddy snickered. "Can't get rid of *you* by taking a Bromo!"

"Damn!" Frankie's annoyance made him blink more rapidly than usual. "Why doesn't this gagger hire himself an audience? And I wish the police would get here. These amateurs make me sick!" And his glare, transferred from Buddy to Jack, made no bones about what he meant.

"O.K.," said Buddy, reaching into his pocket and throwing Jack a dime. "Here's your retainer, as they say in books. Oh— I forgot! You were a professional. Give me back that dime!"

Jack was becoming confused. Nothing was working out the way it should. They were all against him. It was just like fighting a pillow—little real opposition, but it got you no place. Well, there was at least one person he could work on.

"Jimmy!" he exclaimed suddenly, turning on the boy, and feeling like the district attorney in a Grade B movie. "You'd better tell us what you know—unless, of course, you're too deeply involved—" He paused suggestively.

"Why pick on me? I don't know anything," answered Jimmy, his eyes fixed firmly on the ever-present cigarette between his fingers.

"I think you do," Jack said. "When I came into your room this morning, you told a cock-and-bull story about Tony wanting to sleep in another room. And yet he left his pajamas in your room. Besides which he was killed in his tux. So you'll have to tell a better story than that."

"I didn't kill him!" Jimmy cried. "Wh-why should I?"

Jack caught Windy's eye. Windy nodded.

"You know, Jimmy," Jack went on, "that your room and ours are connected by the common bathroom?"

"So what?"

"Just this: Last night, Windy and I overheard your quarrel with Tony. I may as well tell you that we heard enough to give you motives for killing both Andy and Tony."

"I—I don't know what you're talking about!" Jimmy denied.

"All right. You asked for it!" Jack took a deep breath.

"Item: You forged Andy's name to a check. Andy discovered it, and threatened you with exposure and jail. Motive for Andy's murder.

"Item: Tony has the check—or, I should say—*had* the check, and attempted to blackmail you for it. Motive for Tony's murder. Well—?"

Jimmy looked down at his hands, saw that they were trembling, and put them quickly in his pockets. The silence became too much for him to bear, so he finally looked up, and said:

"All right, so you heard it! I needed money, so I did forge a check, but a great deal of Andy's money is really mine."

"What do you mean, yours?"

"It's kind of a long story. You see, my mother, who was my father's second wife, left a lot of money when she died. Since she died before my father did, she naturally left everything to him, assuming that he'd take care of me. But when he died, soon afterward, he left everything to Andy, expecting that my mother's money would be held in trust for me until I was of age. But he didn't know Andy. Andy packed me off to a boarding school, and used that money to start the band. I never got anything of what was coming to me. Andy denied that any of it was rightly mine. I was helpless legally. So I didn't have any compunction about forging a check when I needed some cash. But that doesn't mean I killed Tony for the check. Iggy had a fight with him too, and didn't he accuse Max, and Lee, as well as Iggy?"

"True, but you had an excellent opportunity to do just as you pleased. After we overhear a violent quarrel between you two, Tony is found dead, downstairs. How did he get there? Did you kill him in your room, then carry his body down to divert suspicion from yourself?"

"I didn't do it!" Jimmy's face was contorted with rage. Jack suddenly remembered reading somewhere that an angry man is a frightened man. "I didn't kill him," Jimmy repeated, "even though I can't prove that I didn't."

"Well, then, tell us all you know. You must know something about it."

"All right," Jimmy agreed, becoming tractable, "This is what happened last night:" He started his story with a great show of candor.

"Last night, after we had that fight, Tony was kind of sore. I called him a blackmailer, and all that. He didn't speak to me after that, and I didn't feel so friendly toward him either. I undressed, and got into bed. I thought he'd change his mind, eventually, about bleeding me. And besides, the longer I put him off, the more chance there was of the real murderer being discovered, so that Tony couldn't hold that check over me any longer." Jimmy took a deep breath, as if relieved at getting his story off his mind. "Tony didn't undress at all, just kept sitting on a chair, reading a magazine and smoking. The light bothered me, and I couldn't fall asleep with it on, so I finally asked him if he was waiting up for Santa Claus, or what? But he ignored me completely—didn't answer at all. So after a while, I finally fell asleep.

"Sometime later, a knock on the door woke me up. That is, I suppose I heard a knock, because I saw Tony, still dressed, go to the door, and open it a crack. He spoke to someone there in a low voice, but I couldn't hear what was said. I was half asleep anyhow. Then Tony went out. I called after him to ask where he was going, and he called back: 'Downstairs.' I wanted to know what for, but he just whispered back something like 'Mind your own business!' I looked at my watch. It was just one-thirty when he left, so I minded my own business and went back to sleep. I didn't wake up till this morning, and I had just noticed that Tony's bed hadn't been slept in at all when you walked in. And that's all I know!" Jimmy concluded defiantly.

"Ha! A likely story!" Frankie scoffed.

"It's true," Jimmy insisted. "And you can like it or lump it!"

"Could be!" Buddy said judiciously. "Maybe Tony had to see a dog about a man."

Jack looked thoughtfully at Jimmy, endeavoring to separate the truth from the fiction. It was possible that something like that had happened. Jimmy couldn't have killed Tony in their room, because the sound of the shot would have penetrated through the bathroom door. But how, then, could Jimmy have induced Tony, still dressed, to go downstairs to his death?

Suppose, though, that Tony did know who the killer was, as he had insinuated in that conversation they had overheard. And suppose, too, that Tony had tried a little blackmail in that direction, since it was too good an opportunity to overlook. So he and the murderer had arranged a meeting in the lounge late at night, when there was no danger of being either interrupted or overheard. Then suppose that the killer had decided that since he was in for one murder, another wouldn't matter so much, especially since an immediate danger to his safety would be removed. It was a logical explanation, if Jimmy's story were true. Jack pulled at his lower lip, wondering who had been at that door.

"You didn't hear the voice of the person who called for Tony?" he asked finally.

"No," answered Jimmy. "All I heard was whispering." The other occupants of the lounge were now viewing Jimmy with undisguised suspicion. His friction with Tony and Andy was evidently news to them. Jimmy felt this antagonistic wave of feeling, and looked about him in alarm.

Then, feeling that Jack was his strongest ally, he asked weakly: "You do believe me, don't you?"

Jack's answer was blunt. "As far as you go, yes. The trouble is you don't go far enough. You haven't told us yet what happened to that check."

"How should I know what happened to it?"

"You know, because you obtained it sometime between last night and this morning."

Again that look of fear flitted across Jimmy's face, "I—I guess Tony still has it," he stammered.

"I guess not!" Jack asserted. "You burned it last night in your ash tray, didn't you?"

"How do you know?"

"Those ashes in your ash tray weren't entirely from cigarettes. There's only one thing that might incriminate you enough to make it necessary for you to destroy it, and that's the check. So you'd better tell us the rest of that story."

"I—er—found the check in Tony's bureau drawer among his things," Jimmy said sullenly after a pregnant pause.

"No you didn't! You found it in Tony's billfold!" Jack's voice cut sharply through the cigarette haze dimming the room. The others listened breathlessly to this exchange. And they eyed Jack with considerably more respect than he had commanded up to then.

"When you took it from his wallet," Jack cracked the question suddenly, "was Tony alive—or dead?"

"He was dead," Jimmy replied as if hypnotized.

"Did you kill him?"

Jimmy tried to speak, but his mouth was too dry, and only a cracked sound emerged.

"Listen to me, Jimmy," Jack said, a little more kindly. "You'll do much better if you tell us the truth—the whole truth. Pieces of it won't help, if you're innocent. If you're not—well, then it's too bad for you, and you have the legal right to refuse to tell us anything that might incriminate you. It's up to you."

"I'll tell you everything," Jimmy said finally.

"Is it true that someone came to the door for Tony?"

"Yes, it is," Jimmy said earnestly. "Only—well, when Tony left, I thought I'd use that opportunity to look for that check. I hunted through all his things, turned the room inside out, but no check. I really didn't expect to find it. Tony would know that I'd search for it in our room the minute his back was turned. I kept expecting him back any minute. It took me a while to replace his things the way he'd left them. I didn't want him to know that I'd looked for it. Then, about a half hour after he had left, I became curious—wondered why he hadn't returned. So I decided to go down to see where he was, and what he was doing."

"Weren't you afraid you'd be in danger if Tony caught you snooping after him?" Jack interrupted to ask. "For all you knew, he might have been the murderer."

"I was so worried about that check that I didn't even think of it," confessed Jimmy. "And somehow, I never suspected Tony of having killed Andy."

"No," agreed Iggy. "Tony was more the type to get something on someone. His motto was let them live, and make them suffer."

"What happened then?" asked Buddy, for once sitting quietly, and listening enthralled.

"When I came to the lounge," Jimmy continued, "I opened the door very quietly. I saw a light there, so I listened to try to hear what they were saying. When I didn't hear a sound, I pushed the door wide open. Tony— Tony was sitting there—looking at me—his eyes open . . ."

Jack suddenly visualized the sight he and Iggy had come upon that morning, and he almost shuddered in company with Jimmy.

"Then Tony was dead when you discovered him?"

"Yes. I swear he was!" Jimmy's face was bloodless as the scene with all its dread horror returned to his memory. And there was a ring of sincerity in his voice that had to be believed. "He—the body was still warm, and that—that little hole in his head—with the eyes staring—staring at me . . . Oh, it was horrible!"

The others sighed, living the horror over again with him. Lee sat with her hand over her eyes, her mouth a tense red line.

"And so you searched him for the check?" Jack asked, finally breaking the silence.

"Yes. I don't know how I had the nerve to do it, when I think about it now. But last night—it was just like being in a nightmare. I didn't feel anything. All I thought of was that I simply had to get that check before the police got here." Jimmy buried his face in his hands.

"You went right upstairs as soon as you got the check?" Jack felt like an inquisitor forcing Jimmy to answer.

"Yes. And I burned it the minute I got to my room. Then I realized what had happened. That for all I knew the murderer was hidden somewhere around, and might have seen me searching Tony. I didn't know what to do. I lay awake all night, wondering whether I ought to tell the rest of you. Then I decided not to. To let someone else discover the body. I was afraid I'd be suspected if you found I'd discovered Tony that way in the middle of the night."

"If Windy and I hadn't heard you arguing with Tony, we'd never have known anything about it," Jack mused. "And you know, Jimmy, you should have put that card back in Tony's wallet, and the wallet back where it had been."

Jimmy's color was better now, and he looked almost normal again. "I suppose I just wasn't cut out to be a criminal," he said with a weak attempt at a smile.

Jack was inclined to agree with him. Jimmy's nervous demeanor was entirely at variance with the coolness the murderer has thus far displayed. He thought about the salient points in Jimmy's tale. If Jimmy had spoken the truth, Tony had been murdered sometime between one-thirty and two in the morning. Which definitely cleared both Max and Lee.

What a screwball case! The only two people who could have killed Andy were the two who couldn't have killed Tony!

# 14

The door opened, interrupting Jack's disheartened review of the situation, and in walked Si with an elaborately decorated Spanish guitar under one arm. His eyes were bleary and bloodshot, and his thick mouth had a wry twist, as if he had just tasted vinegar. He was very obviously in the more painful throes of a hangover.

"Leaving for the week-end, Si?" Buddy asked him casually.

"What do you mean?" Si peered at him with one eye closed, as if it took too much effort for him to open both at the same time.

"I see you have the bags under your eyes packed."

"Ouch!" Si winced, and pushed a stray lock of blond hair off his face. "That's all I needed! I think I'd better get drunk again, so I won't have to listen to cracks like that. Incidentally," he said, looking around the room, "was Andy sore about last night? I mean about my getting drunk? Bet he gives me hell for it."

"Andy won't give you hell," Frankie commented. "Someone gave it to *him*—just presented the whole place to him for his future use."

"Now you're cooking with gas, brother!" Buddy said joyously.

"Oh, stop talking like a Hollywood imitation of a musician!" Frankie snapped irritably.

Si's glance fell on Jack and Windy. He peered at them through half shut lids, trying to get them in focus.

"So our band had two blessed events, eh?" he said.

"Meet Benny Goodman and Harpo Marx," Buddy announced gleefully. "They have already had the pleasure of meeting you, but in your—er—delicate condition."

"Pleased to meetcha, Benny; pleased to meetcha, Harpo," Si said, shaking hands with them cordially.

Windy threw Jack a weary look which said plainly: What a bunch of characters!

"I'd like to ask you some questions, Si," said Jack, "if you don't mind."

"Oh, my goodness!" Si exclaimed in amazement. "I thought Harpo couldn't talk!"

"Si's I.Q.: thirty-nine and a half," Buddy said, winking at Jack.

"My name's Jack, and this is Windy. We arrived last night, while you were—er—sleeping . . ."

"Don't be so polite," Si said, grinning good-naturedly. "Just say while I was drunk. You won't hurt my feelings, if that's what you're afraid of. Everyone has an escape of some sort. Mine is liquor. Cheaper than a lot of other things." And his eyebrows waggled up and down suggestively.

Jack tried to size this broad-boned chap up. He looked like a husky farm lad, but his diction was cultured and precise, and at complete variance with the lax disregard of the niceties of grammar affected by his fellow musicians.

"Don't bother giving Si the third degree, Jack," Buddy advised shrewdly. "He already has it—a Ph.D. in economics. He knows how to balance the budget for the New Deal, but they don't believe him, so he's lucky he can play that guitar. Else he'd be on relief now."

"I'd just as lief be on relief!" Si said, improvising a melody on his guitar. "Let's see now." He shook his head gingerly to clear it, then winced with pain. "Oh, I remember. You didn't tell me what Andy said about me. Come on, spill the bad news. Am I canned? And say, where is Precious, by the way?"

"Andy and Tony are dead. They were murdered last night." Jack watched the guitarist carefully to see what effect his bald statement would have on him. There was no appreciable effect.

"Really?" Si continued picking out chords, unmoved. "So someone got a brainstorm, eh? Well, it's about time," he concluded indifferently.

"Do you know anything about it?" Jack asked, ready to throw in the towel.

"Me? No! Maybe the exterminator did it in his regular line of duty. Exterminators can occasionally be very conscientious." Then Si paused, his brow furrowed as if he were doing some heavy thinking.

"Let me get this straight," he said finally. "Those two excrescences, those two blots on humanity were rubbed out, and you don't know to whom to award the D.S.C.?"

"Get that 'to whom' business," Buddy whispered proudly. "The guy has class!"

"That's right," Jack said in answer to Si. "Andy was shot while he was singing last night, shot from behind. Tony was shot after we went to bed, in the lounge. Can you shed any light on the matter?"

"Who is suspected?" Si asked.

"Everyone."

"Did Andy say anything about me before he was so rudely cut off in his crime—er, beg pardon—his prime of life?"

"And how!" Buddy chuckled. "He was in rare form last night. He out-Andied Andy, if you know what I mean."

"That means I have a motive," Si ruminated. "I might have killed him because he fired me. Which makes me a suspect too. Just one of the boys—that's me!"

"That's *I*," whispered Buddy.

"You can't say I'm not democratic," Si continued. "I did it while I was intoxicated, eh?"

"No," admitted Jack with a sigh. "You're out. Andy didn't fire you, just docked you a week's pay. Not much of a motive. Besides which you're practically the only one who couldn't have committed either crime—unless you were faking that jag of yours."

"He'd have to be some actor to paint that hangover on his face!"

"What do you mean, hangover, Buddy?" Si asked with an injured look. "I always look like this. All right—so I ain't cute! But if I'm out as a suspect, then you'll have to look for the butler. In every book I ever read, it was always the butler."

"O.K.," Iggy commented sardonically. "We'll have to wait until Max hires a butler."

"Of course, if you really want to know who the murderer is," Si said thoughtfully, "you can always get a copy of Winchell's column. He'll tell you. He sees all, hears all, and gets paid a-plenty for telling it."

"Si," Lee broke in seriously, "don't be so flippant. Two people have been murdered, and whether we liked them or not, we've got to help Jack discover the murderer. He's not doing this just for his benefit, you know."

If Jack had had any doubts of his being in love with Lee before this, he lost them now. She was definitely the girl for him.

Si took her reproof good-naturedly. "Sorry, Lee. You're absolutely right, of course. But I'm afraid I can't help. I don't know a thing. So help me, I could have killed both of them, and I still wouldn't know it."

"Wish the rest of us had your alibi," Iggy said morosely. "You weren't on the bandstand when Andy was shot, and as for Tony's murder, Frankie said you were snoring all night—disturbed his beauty sleep."

Si surveyed Frankie with undisguised interest. "You mean it's my fault he looks like that?" He shook his head pityingly and sighed. He began fingering his guitar again.

"Hey, you cats, how about a little jive?" he asked, the subject of the murders evidently exhausted as far as he was concerned. "I worked out a couple of breaks for *Lady Be Good* that are solid senders. Come on, Ig—get in the groove, and give out with those chords—in E flat, please."

Iggy turned to the piano, complying with relief. In this he was on solid ground. Si began picking out the melody with teasing glissandos, making his own peculiar additions—his "breaks."

They listened a while; then Buddy yelled:

"Hey, you guys! Wait for me! I'm horning in on this." And he ran out to the bandstand for his trumpet. He returned instantly, blowing those queer strangled sounds a horn player gets out of his trumpet when warming up.

"Why don't you get your woodpile, Frankie, and join us?" he invited, taking his lips momentarily from the mouthpiece of his instrument.

"Include me out!" Frankie snapped. "This is a helluva time to jam, with two corpses upstairs, and maybe more in the making. And how many times have I asked you not to call my vibraphone a woodpile!"

"Tsk-tsk! Get a load of Frankie, the purist!" Buddy jeered. "He played tympani with the Philharmonic for two weeks, once upon a time, and hasn't recovered yet. O.K., you longhair—sit there and make braids." And they went on without the drummer, while the others gathered round and listened.

The three musicians began swinging away, improvising on the theme and around the basic harmony, weaving an entirely original pattern from the tune. Then as they came around again to the beginning of the song, Lee came in on the vocal of the second chorus, her husky young voice emphasizing the offbeat, setting everyone's feet to tapping.

Max sidled over to Jack, and whispered proudly: "She's strictly from the top drawer, hey?"

Jack agreed wholeheartedly, and he found that his own fingers were itching to do a little bass slapping with the trio, but the thought that he had as yet accomplished nothing toward solving the mystery held him back. He decided that while they were all congregated, he had the chance to do a little sleuthing. If they wouldn't co-operate with him, at least they wouldn't hinder him now. He moved toward Windy, who was tapping his foot with the rest, and whispered: "Hey, Windy, do me a favor?"

"Sure. What?"

"Just keep an eye on these guys for me. I want to search their rooms while they're busy. Perhaps I'll find something that'll help clear this mess up."

"O.K.," agreed Windy, talking expertly out of the side of his mouth. "I'll be a l'il mouse, watching a bunch of hep-cats." And he grinned, his fat face broadening.

Jack walked out to the strains of Lee concluding her chorus, and there was Buddy, taking over again, his horn notes emerging rough and rhythmic.

Max was right, he thought as he entered the quiet of the dance hall. They were all from the top drawer as far as music was concerned. As an outfit, they were tops. But someone in there was literally getting away with murder! Something had to be done about it—and fast! And it appeared as though he were the only one interested in clearing it up, with only Windy willing to co-operate at all. And what did Windy know about the boys? Just about as much as he himself did. Well, now he was in for some dull routine work. Jack went reluctantly, because he would much rather have been in the lounge, listening to Lee singing. He cursed himself for having been born with a conscience.

As he walked up the stairs he continued thinking. So far, he knew exactly nothing. He hadn't the faintest idea who the guilty one could possibly be. He wasn't even certain that only one person was responsible. Maybe two or more were in collusion. He ran over the possibilities.

Frankie—with his nervous motions, his restless ways. Why was he so irritable, so afraid? There was a reefer in the woodpile. Perhaps Tony had refused to sell Frankie any more of the marijuana cigarettes. That might give the drummer a possible motive in Tony's death. But how then would that tie him up with Andy? Andy had been shot first. No, there was no definite evidence pointing toward Frankie, nothing except his jumpy demeanor, which might be explained by a naturally temperamental disposition aggravated by the use of narcotics and whiskey.

Buddy? Buddy had had a fist fight with the band leader before the shooting had occurred, but it was a fight that had apparently arisen from nothing more serious than frayed nerves. But Buddy hated Andy, and he made no bones about this antipathy. Why? Was it really out of sympathy for Iggy, and the wrong Andy had done the pianist? And Buddy had remarked that Andy was always sneering at his —Buddy's—playing. But what kind of motive was that for a murder? That ghoulishness of Buddy's, the malice he displayed in his wisecracks—was it evidence of a streak of hardness, of sadism—or was it actually what Iggy had diagnosed it as being—merely a defense mechanism? Buddy, Jack decided, would bear watching.

And what about Iggy himself? Jack had to admit that the pianist had an excellent motive for killing Andy. The royalties from *Headlined in My Heart* had lined Andy's pockets, and had furthermore had the effect of reviving the public's interest in his band. And though killing Andy didn't return the proceeds from the song to its rightful owner, it would be adequate revenge for the theft. And Tony had prodded Iggy about it after Andy's death. But that wouldn't be motive enough for Iggy to kill Tony too, not unless the saxophonist had had actual proof of Iggy's guilt. But Iggy hadn't been in a position to kill Andy while playing the piano. It would have been impossible from where he had been sitting. And, for that matter, how could any of the band have killed Andy while playing? Jack came up square against this moot point, and turned away from it disheartened. He was getting sick of milling it over and over. . . . He went back to his inventory:

Ray? Bland, inscrutable Ray; never betraying any emotion or surprise. Those thick glasses masked effectively any expression his eyes might reveal. Ray certainly was a cool customer. Yet he had no obvious motive for either murder. No, all Jack knew definitely about Ray was that he was a phenomenal sax player, even though he appeared outwardly too cold to make a good musician. Still, who knew what flames were banked within that cold exterior?

And Si—a Ph.D.—earning his livelihood as a guitarist. What a combination! As a matter of fact, the whole band was an answer to a squirrel's prayer.

Why wasn't Si more curious about what had happened? He couldn't be the killer in either case, although his alibi for the time of Tony's murder did depend to a great extent on Frankie. There was no evidence whatsoever pointing to Si. It was probable that his indifference was just that and nothing more. Si couldn't have killed Andy, and that was that! Jack smiled wryly, thinking that if this were fiction, Si would be the murderer, just *because* he couldn't have done it.

And what about Jimmy, Andy's half-brother? Right now, Jimmy certainly was Public Suspect Number One. He had a motive for Andy's death—money. A motive for Tony's death, as well as a made to order opportunity. Yet somehow Jack felt that the thing didn't stop there. It just didn't jell. If Jimmy had wanted to kill Tony, why had he done it in the lounge? Jimmy had been badly frightened, but only before he had told his story. Well, Jimmy had to be filed away for future reference.

Max? Max had a motive for Andy's death, all right. Kitty was his whole world, and any threat to the safety of that world would be dealt with summarily. And he had had the best opportunity of all to kill Andy. But there was no evidence pointing toward him for Tony's death. He had an alibi for that time. Then again, would Cohen's testimony hold up under scrutiny? A long talk with Cohen was indicated.

And last but not least—Lee! Jack's heart melted with a soft flop at the very thought of her. She made him feel like all the sappy lyrics a songwriter ever dreamed up. Try as he would, he simply couldn't view her objectively. He was tickled silly that Kitty could alibi her for Tony's murder. Even if she had had an opportunity to kill Andy, as well as an acceptable motive, she had neither for Tony.

Well, this thinking wasn't getting him anywhere. He was upstairs now, and he opened one of the bedroom doors and buckled down to work. He searched carefully and methodically, hiding all evidence of his search. He felt like a heel, reading personal mail and going over bills and such, but he assuaged the pangs of his conscience with the thought that it was absolutely necessary.

A half hour later, he dusted off his hands in Jimmy's room, weary but none the wiser. He had gone over the rooms of the remaining musicians in the band, but the sum total of his work was nil—absolutely nothing! The only conclusion he could draw was that Max needed more efficient chambermaids, unless they were lax only about the musicians' rooms. He wondered with great self-contempt how the detectives in novels always managed to uncover such a multitude of clues from practically nothing. He had examined plenty of material, but none of it had had the slightest bearing on the case. As a detective, he was one big flop!

Then Jack decided to take another look through Andy's room—the only room he had skipped in his search. It was possible that Andy had something hidden among his papers.

He opened the door to Andy's room reluctantly. He tiptoed in softly. Then, chiding himself for being such a sissy, he stepped in with his normal stride. With a great show of bravado, he slammed the door shut behind him.

The room was gloomy, even after he put on the electric light. It held an eerie, waiting tension, as if the bodies were aware that this was not their final resting place. He observed them lying side by side, covered with sheets that only suggested the forms underneath, and by that very suggestion was more terrifying than the reality.

He glanced toward the dresser next to Andy's bed, and decided to look through that first.

Hey! Was the spread under Andy's body fluttering?

A fine thing! Now he was seeing things. Nerves, just nerves. What an imagination he had suddenly acquired.

Nevertheless, Jack stood motionless for a moment, his eyes glued to that spread.

There it went again! It *had* fluttered . . . ! This time there was no mistake.

Someone—something—was under that bed!

Jack opened his mouth, but no sound emerged. This was like the familiar nightmare. His feet were rooted fantastically to the floor, and it seemed impossible that he would ever be able to move again. . . .

# 15

Jack stood there for an eternity. Then his courage returned. He stiffened his right forefinger, and stuck it in his jacket pocket so that it protruded. A pretty poor imitation of a gun, he had to admit, both as far as looks and utility were concerned. No self-respecting murderer would be fooled for an instant by it, but it was the best he could do. Jack waited another second, trying to compose himself, then spoke suddenly in a flat voice that persisted in emerging with a quaver:

"Come out of there—or I shoot!"

He almost jumped at the sound of his own voice in the stillness. He hadn't intended to make it so loud, so loud and so woefully unconvincing.

That noise! Why—it sounded suspiciously like a sneeze! There was another—and another—all coming from under the bed.

Someone came scuffling out from under Andy's bed, still sneezing. His face was contorted with the explosive outbursts, and he was covered by cobwebs. His hair was gray with feathery blobs of dust.

As the apparition raised hesitant arms skyward, Jack, emboldened by the success of his ancient ruse, asked sternly:

"Who are you—and what are you doing here?"

"Please don't shoot," begged the dust-covered figure. "I—I'm Barclay Cl—Ah—CHOO!! Clark."

Jack could see that he was young, and as the boy brushed the dust from his face, and the intervals between those agonizing sneezes lengthened, he recognized him with a start of surprise. It was the young medical student, the one who had examined Andy's body right after the bandleader had been shot.

"Aren't you Butch?" Jack asked suddenly.

The boy jumped visibly as the sound of Jack's voice broke the stillness.

"Y-yes," he stammered. "That's what everyone calls m-me. Are—are you going to k-kill me, too?"

"What do you mean—kill you too?"

Butch nodded toward Tony's sheet-covered body. "You killed him, didn't you?"

Jack stood dumbfounded before this accusation, "Me?" he asked in amazement. "Why, you dumb cluck, I didn't kill anyone! What makes you think I did?"

Disbelief replaced the terror on Butch's young face. "Oh, no? Then what's Tony doing here dead, if you didn't kill him? And what are you doing here gloating over the bodies? And where did you get that gun in your pocket? Tell me that!" the boy flung at him defiantly.

Jack collapsed on a convenient chair, weak with laughter. So this was the much vaunted sophistication of the new generation! Hoodwinked by a finger in a pocket!

"And I thought the murderer was under the bed!" he gulped, "I was sure my last hour had come."

Butch eyed the empty hand Jack displayed. Suspicion, bewilderment, and finally relief followed in quick succession over his countenance.

"I'm Jack Coler," said Jack, when his mirth had subsided.

"Yeah, I know—the bass player. I saw you with the band last night. Oh, I remember now—one of the musicians said you were a detective, too. Whew! You sure did scare me to death!"

"Me too!" Jack said fervently, as he wiped his damp forehead. "I'm the only one interested in clearing this thing up, and you take me for the murderer!"

"But how did Tony get up here? And with that hole in his head? Who did that?"

"The same one who gave Andy his, I guess. Iggy and I found him dead in the lounge this morning. He was evidently murdered late last night. Everyone is downstairs in the lounge now, so I thought it would be my opportunity to do some clue-hunting. Incidentally, what are you doing here?"

"Well—" Butch hesitated—"Kitty was so broken up about this—about Andy, I mean—and I thought that if I could only solve it, she'd respect me more. Damn! Why do women have to go for men twice their own age, anyway!" he burst out bitterly, "She thinks I'm not dry behind the ears yet, and I'm twenty-one—three years older than she is. She thinks I'm just a kid. With her, love begins at forty, and up! Anyone under that still needs didies as far as she's concerned. Gosh—don't women make you sick, though!"

Jack tried hard to keep from laughing at the boy's earnestness. "Yes," he agreed, the corners of his mouth twitching in spite of himself, "women are the limit. So you thought that if you unmasked Andy's murderer, Kitty would be eternally grateful to you. Is that it?"

"Well, flowers and candy don't register with Kitty." Butch shook his head in despair. "I don't have the past to suit her. I cut all my classes to come here just to see her, but she'll dance with me and make eyes at Andy. I ought to grow a beard or something to look older; then maybe she'd give me a tumble."

He looked so woebegone that Jack really felt sorry for him. Love affairs weren't successful in the Log House. First the Abbott girl, then Iggy, and now Butch.

"Don't worry about it," Jack tried to console him. "That's just a stage she's going through. She'll grow out of it eventually. And if you're around when she needs you— well, she'll grow to depend on you and care for you."

"You really think so?" Butch asked hopefully.

"I'm certain of it. By the way, did you discover anything in your search?"

"Nah!" Butch admitted despondently, "This may be an open and shut case, but it's just shut as far as I'm concerned. I tried examining the wounds, but all I can tell is that the same gun—or rather, the same type of gun killed both Andy and Tony. It was a gun of small caliber. You can see the size of the bullet more clearly by Tony's wound. Andy's is too bloody the way it is now to tell much. The medical examiner will be able to get much more information from the bodies, as well as the bullets. I can't deduce much from the simple examination I can give them. What I was really looking for, though, was the gun. That's the most important clue right now."

"I had the same idea," Jack said. "Only the gun isn't around. Oh, I'm getting sick and tired of making like a detective. Frankie was right when he said this was no case for amateurs. I wish the phone company would repair those wires that blew down, so we could get some expert attention."

"Wires blew down?" Butch asked curiously. "What do you mean? They were cut!"

"Cut! Are you sure?"

"Positive! The phones all over the hotel, as well as the one in Mr. Harris' office and the pay phone booths near the bar, were put out of commission intentionally. I examined every one in the joint, but not a single one was overlooked."

Jack cursed his stupidity. "What a fool I am! I should have guessed that's what would happen."

"This is how I figure it," Butch said importantly, pleased at the turn events had taken, putting him in the position of giving important information to the detective in the case.

"The wires were probably blown down to begin with, and that played into the murderer's hands so well that he decided to make sure the police wouldn't arrive too soon— at least not as long as the storm made going for help impractical. The longer the length of time between the crime and questioning, the easier it is for eyewitnesses to forget exactly what happened. Especially since such reports are usually inaccurate to begin with—Psychology Five: The Psychology of the Witness," he concluded proudly.

"This is some kettle of herring," Jack mused. "Now what?"

"We find the murderer ourselves," Butch said nonchalantly. "We have an advantage over the police in that we were right at the scene of the crime. So all we have to do is apply any knowledge we have to the facts in the case."

"That all? Ha ha!" Jack laughed hollowly. "What do you think I've been trying to do till now? And I still don't know a darn thing. Oh, well, let's go to Max's office. I want to see how those wires were cut. Not that it'll do us much good to know, though. Say," he continued, as they went down, "you didn't happen to kill Andy, did you, Butch? You have a good motive."

"Who, me?" Butch was startled. "Why should I kill him?"

"Kitty means a great deal to you, as you've been telling me," Jack explained half-jokingly. "And if Andy were cutting in seriously, as was the case—well, men have been killed for less."

"Ha!" Butch laughed bitterly. "If I had to kill every old jerk that Kitty got a crush on—I'd be kept busier than Dracula in a blood bank!"

"You mean she's been that way before?"

"Oh, sure! She gets a yen for almost every bandleader that Mr. Harris hires. It's not the men themselves, so much, I guess; it's the glamor, and all that. If all those society dames fall in droves for bandleaders, you can't blame Kitty for doing the same thing."

"So you just keep waiting for her current crush to run its course?"

"Yep, that's me—Old Faithful."

"In other words, you claim that you have no motive, eh, Butch?"

"That's right," Butch answered placidly. "Besides, I have an alibi. I was dancing with Kitty out front when Andy was killed."

"I know," Jack admitted wearily. "The one thing I'm certain of is that Andy's murderer was on the bandstand when Andy was shot."

They entered Max's office. Jack examined the phone, wires, and reaffirmed Butch's conclusion. They had been severed near the base of the phone box on the lower part of the wall, which accounted for the fact that Jack hadn't noticed it in the morning.

Jack opened the top drawer of Max's desk, while Butch watched him with ill-concealed interest. The revolver was still there, untouched, and gleaming coldly, and right near it was a large pair of efficient shears that looked ugly in their utilitarian way.

"That's what was used to cut those telephone wires," Butch said. "But Mr. Harris always kept them in the second drawer."

"Finding them doesn't help us much," Jack said. "All the boys in the band would have known about them."

He examined the painted black handles, shiny, smooth, and unblemished. Not a fingerprint on them.

"You bet all the fellows in the band knew about them," Butch agreed. "They were in here more than Mr. Harris— always running in for adhesive tape, or first aid for a finger, or Scotch tape to mend torn sheet music."

Jack looked carefully through the other drawers. The one at the very bottom was filled to overflowing with college pamphlets. He examined them all, noting that in the catalogue of the University of Michigan was a letter from the registrar of that college, admitting one Katherine Harris to the University for the Spring semester.

Jack fingered the catalogue. "So Max was telling the truth about sending Kitty away," he said aloud. "This letter proves it, and weakens his motive."

"You didn't really suspect him?" Butch asked apprehensively. "Mr. Harris wouldn't murder anyone. Why, he's the softest-hearted person you'd ever want to meet."

"Max is a suspect, nevertheless," Jack said. "He admits that he hated Andy, and he had the best opportunity in the world to kill him, which is more than I can say for the others."

"Gosh!" Butch exclaimed. "Kitty is acting broken up about Andy's death. But if I know Kitty, and I ought to by now, a lot of it is just acting. She likes the limelight, and this tragic heroine pose appeals to her. But if her father were really in danger—well, I'd hate to be around!"

"I wouldn't worry about it," Jack assured him. "The evidence against Max is far from conclusive. Gets weaker all the time, as a matter of fact. Well, I'm going back to the lounge. You get back to Kitty, and see if she knows anything. Andy may have let something slip to her."

"Right!" Butch's eyes shone at this evidence of his acceptance as an official assistant.

They walked down the dance floor, Butch hard put to keep up with Jack's long-legged stride. Suddenly both saw a shadowy figure moving out from the entrance leading to the hotel.

"Kitty!" Butch exclaimed, and he hastened his steps, catching up with her near the bandstand. He held her arm, although she tried to break away from his grasp, saying petulantly:

"You leave me alone, Butch!"

"What are you doing here?" he asked, continuing to hold her fast. "Didn't your father tell you not to leave the hotel?"

Jack caught up with them. He saw that Kitty's face was just as heavily made up as the night before. She was dressed in a long, elaborately quilted silk housecoat with wide, kimono-like sleeves. There were rings under her blue eyes, but it was impossible to tell whether they were due to too much eyeshadow, or to lack of sleep. She appeared even younger than she had the night before. Her head bent back so that she could look at Jack's face so far above her, she smiled impertinently and said:

"Butch, who is this gentleman? I don't believe we've met."

"This is Jack, Honey," Butch said. "He's trying to solve Andy's murder. He will, too, I bet."

"Oh, yes." Kitty's voice was cordial, and she fluttered her mascara-coated lashes. "Lee was telling me about you."

"What did she say?" Jack couldn't help asking.

"Oh," Kitty drawled with a coy inflection, "she said you were kind of nice—and smart, too."

Jack was sure that a jigger of good rye had been poured into him unaware. Where else did that glow come from?

"Come on, Kitty," said Butch, putting a protective arm about her, "you'd better go back to the hotel. I'll come along, and we'll have a nice long talk. Maybe you can help Jack. You may know something you don't know you know."

"What do you mean—something I know I don't know—er—I know I know—er—" Kitty floundered. "What I'm trying to say is that I do know something," she finally said, her voice echoing shrilly in the great empty hall. "I know something *important!*" And she flung her arms out in a theatrical gesture, judging the action of her long flowing sleeves to a nicety.

She thinks this whole affair is something staged for her benefit, thought Jack, watching her. This murder was something to give her a chance to display her histrionic talent. She probably had the lead in the school play.

Kitty glanced furtively about the room. Then, deciding that no one was eavesdropping, she lowered her voice and whispered:

"*I know who killed Andy!*"

In spite of himself, Jack felt cold chills run up and down his spine.

"What do you mean?" he asked quickly, breathlessly.

"If all of you weren't so dumb," she said scornfully, "you'd have guessed."

"Perhaps you're right," Jack agreed. "But hurry and tell us what you know. Delay may be dangerous."

"The whole band was jealous of Andy," Kitty continued, refusing to be hurried. "Jealous of his success, of his wonderful personality, of his talent, and of his popularity with everyone." Jack took that one with a pound of salt.

"But—" she looked about the dance hall again—"but there is only one person here who hated him enough to kill him—and that was Tony!" she concluded with the effect of having thrown a bombshell at them.

"But, Kitty—" Butch protested.

"Wait a minute, Butch," Jack interrupted him. "Tell us how you know, Kitty."

"Andy himself told me so," she answered triumphantly. "It was the day before yesterday, and we were eating together in one of the cabins. It was nice and cozy, but I could see that Andy was upset. I asked him what the matter was, and he said he'd just had another argument with Tony, but he wouldn't tell me what about. All he said was that I shouldn't be surprised if a knife was found in his—Andy's—back some day; and if it was, I'd know who put it there."

"But Andy was killed by a gun—not a knife," Jack pointed out.

"Oh, what's the difference how he was killed?" she said impatiently. "You don't have to be so technical."

Jack thought about it. Tony was the type to use a knife. That was true. He continued gazing right through Kitty, wondering if it were possible that Tony had killed Andy, and then someone had killed Tony for something that was totally irrelevant to Andy's death.

"And anyway," continued Kitty, becoming restive under Jack's scrutiny, "Tony used to be a knife thrower in a circus. So he would use a knife. Are you sure Andy was shot?"

"Kitty!" Butch exclaimed in exasperation. "Don't be so dumb! You heard the shot yourself. Maybe I'm not such a helluva medical student, but I certainly know enough to tell the difference between a bullet hole and a knife wound!"

"Where were you going now, Kitty?" Jack asked, feeling sorry for Butch.

"I was going in there to accuse Tony," Kitty said defiantly. "I'm not going to let him get away with murder, even if you don't care. Andy shall be avenged!" And she started stalking toward the lounge.

"Look, Angel," said Butch, sighing with long-suffering patience, "come up to the hotel. It won't do you any good to go there. You see, Tony is dead, too. He was murdered just like Andy, so that he can't possibly be the murderer himself."

Kitty pursed her lips at this information.

"That's funny," she said. Then her face lit up again. "Oh, I know! Maybe Tony was overcome with remorse because he stabbed Andy, so he stabbed himself too."

"But I told you, An-dy was shot," Butch repeated wearily, "and so was To-ny! Come with me, like a good girl, and I'll explain it all to you again." And he led her away, unresisting this time, to Jack's great relief.'

Whew! The difference between that dame and Gracie Allen was that Gracie Allen was that way on purpose. Well, Butch knew what he was letting himself in for. What love could do!

He walked up the platform steps reluctantly. Now he'd have to start asking those questions again, trying to dig some information out of the close-mouthed musicians. If he only knew where to start—

His eye fell on a scarlet blotch near one of the instrument stands on the right end of the platform. He kept looking at the spot of brightness in idle curiosity as he approached. It resembled a scarf or a woolly sweater!

He hastened his walk, and his heart sank in an agony of apprehension.

It was Lee, lying there, her eyes closed, her head against one of the chairs. . . .

# 16

Jack's numb brain registered the slight but regular rise and fall of the scarlet sweater. So she was still alive! His knees felt as though they had turned to water, but when he tried to kneel, they became, mysteriously, steel ramrods. He managed to drop down beside her, to feel her pulse. He fumbled frantically among the bones of the slender wrist, and his sigh of thankfulness when he located the weak throbbing was almost a sob. His eyes focused properly again, and he saw that Lee looked as though she had only just dropped off into a deep sleep.

The strain had probably been too much for her. Being cooped up in a madhouse with a murderer loose was no joke. She must have fainted.

His glance fell on the trumpet lying near Lee. He wondered idly what the instrument was doing on the floor. Ray's had been in its case on his chair, the last he had seen of it, and Buddy had been playing on his own in the lounge.

Just then Lee moved slightly. She moaned—a soft, hardly perceptible sound—and her slim white hand moved slowly to her head. She whimpered again.

Jack realized with a shock what that trumpet on the floor meant. Lee had been assaulted with it! And with murderous intent! The heavy brass instrument could easily kill someone.

He stifled his first impulse to call for help. Perhaps he was being over-imaginative, over-cautious, but he wasn't taking any chances with Lee. Mr. X wasn't going to finish the job he had started on her!

Jack gathered Lee up in his arms. She was quiet, now, and still unconscious. As he picked her up, Lee's long black hair brushed his cheek. A wave of tenderness for her rushed over him. She was so light in his arms, so defenseless. He vowed that the one who had hurt Lee would pay for it, no matter what happened.

With the girl in his arms, it was difficult for Jack to push aside the curtain and open the door to her dressing room. Afterwards, he had no recollection of how he managed to do it. Right now he was frantic with worry, afraid that the blow on her head would prove to be serious.

Jack laid her down carefully on the couch. He opened doors frantically, and finally, after uncovering what seemed to him to be an infinity of closets, he found the door to the washroom. He doused a towel he found there in cold water, and hastened back. He washed Lee's forehead with it, and wrapped it about her head. Then he chafed her wrists helplessly.

Lee's face remained tranquil, marble-pale, her eyes still closed. She needed a doctor's attention. Jack's heart contracted at the realization of his complete helplessness. Perhaps Butch would know what to do. But Jack didn't intend leaving that room, not for a minute, not even to call Butch. In the movies, someone always provided smelling salts for emergencies like this, but where on earth did one find smelling salts? And what did they look like? Jack hadn't the faintest conception. He decided after a moment to look for them, and he dashed back to the washroom, searching frantically through the mysterious contents of the medicine chest. Only perfumed odors arose from the contents of the jars and bottles he opened. Nothing that even faintly resembled smelling salts was there. He hesitated, then filled a glass with plain cold water, and went back.

Lee's eyes were open, and filled with bewilderment. When she saw Jack coming toward her, she tried to rise, but fell right back with her hand to her head. With infinite relief, Jack came quickly to her side.

He tried to pick her up, to help her drink the water, but remembrance seemed to rush over her, for she pushed him away with a wordless cry. He noticed then that she eyed the glass in his hand with terror. So she thought that he was the one who had assaulted her, and that he was now trying to finish the job by forcing her to drink poison. Well, he couldn't blame her too much. After all, what did she know about him?

"Don't be afraid of me, Lee," he said gently. "It's only water—I swear it is."

But she turned her head away again when he tried to give it to her.

He had an inspiration. "Look, Lee—I'll drink some of it." And he did, about a quarter of the glass. "That proves it's all right, doesn't it? Now please drink the rest of it. It'll do you good,"

Lee allowed him to hold the glass to her lips, while his other hand supported her in back. She sipped the water, then lay back again, her eyes still on him watchfully.

"Feel better now?" he asked.

She nodded, then winced as the motion hurt her head. She put her hand up, feeling gingerly among the curly strands of hair.

"My head!" she exclaimed weakly. "I feel a lump coming on!"

Jack wet the towel again, and put it on the spot she had indicated.

"There. That'll help keep it down. Do you feel well enough to tell me what happened?"

Her eyes turned wary again. "Are you sure *you* don't know what happened?"

"I didn't know a thing until I found you unconscious. If I had wanted to—to kill you, I could have finished the job easily enough before you returned to consciousness."

She looked at him doubtfully. Jack caught her unresponsive hand in his big one, and held it fast.

"Listen to me, Lee," he said urgently. "I know I've only just met you—although it does seem like a century since yesterday. But—but I'm crazy about you. The minute I saw you, I fell like a ton of bricks. WHAM!—just like that! I'm not much on this romance angle, but you must believe that I'm telling the truth. So do you think I'd do anything to hurt you?"

"I don't know what to think," she said listlessly. "I suppose you wouldn't hurt me, but—but I don't know whom I can trust here . . ."

"You can trust me, Lee," Jack said earnestly. "You must trust me. And you must do whatever you can to help me uncover the truth. Will you?"

The color was flowing back into her cheeks, and she looked nearer normal.

"I believe you," she said gravely. "I don't know why I should, really. But I do."

Jack was almost dizzy with happiness. She had every reason to suspect him, yet she trusted him!

"Then tell me whatever you know," he urged. "Everything, no matter how unimportant it seems to you. Begin with how you happened to be on the platform."

Her full dark eyebrows nearly approached each other in her efforts to concentrate, to remember accurately.

"Let me see, now—oh, I know. I was chilly in the lounge, and I decided to get a jacket I keep in here. I stepped out on the bandstand, and I was almost across it, right near the door to my room, when I felt a faint tickling sensation on my leg, that to a girl always means a run in her silk stocking. I bent down automatically to look, and suddenly I saw stars! Literally. There was a loud pounding in my ears, and I was sure my eardrums would break. Then everything turned black. When I opened my eyes I saw you coming toward me with a glass in your hand. That's why I thought that you—that you—"

"... that I was the fiend in human form," Jack concluded for her. "I'll never forget that moment when I found you lying there outstretched. I was sure you were done for. Don't ever do that to me again," he finished sternly.

"I won't," she dimpled. "Your face was a sight! I thought you were going to burst into tears. It was the most convincing testimonial to your innocence."

"Getting down to business," Jack said seriously, "you didn't see who came up behind you?"

"No, I didn't. I'm sure I'd remember if I had. All I felt was that blow on my head. But I didn't see a thing except those stars, and I saw enough to furnish a planetarium."

"What about the boys in the lounge? Were they still playing when you left?"

"No, they'd stopped quite a while before that. Buddy decided he was hungry for a change, and he walked out with some of the others. They were headed for the kitchen."

"Did Buddy have his trumpet with him, or didn't you notice?"

"Yes, he did," Lee answered. "You know how Buddy is, either eating or cutting up, so now he pretended he was a drum major, and his trumpet was his baton. He marched out of the lounge, waving it around, making like a drum major—you know, picking his knees 'way up, then putting them down pigeon-toed in a very exaggerated fashion." Lee smiled at the memory, then winced again with pain as her head throbbed. Jack took the cue, and put fresh water on the towel.

"Why did you ask about Buddy's trumpet?" she asked curiously, while he was adjusting the towel on her head.

"Because that's what gave you this fancy headache," he replied absently. "I found it on the floor right next to you. It's still there."

Lee's eyes dilated with horror. "You don't think Buddy— Why?"

"I don't know," Jack answered wearily. "But I do know that that run in your stocking probably saved your life. If you hadn't bent down to look at it when you did—well, you wouldn't be worrying about a headache now." He tried to pass the remark off flippantly, but the mere thought of what might have happened made him shudder. He was certainly all out for bigger and better runs in stockings from now on.

"Buddy wouldn't hurt me!" Lee insisted. "He's not like that."

"Because it was Buddy's trumpet that hit you doesn't necessarily mean that he was the one who swung it," Jack reminded her. "Buddy might have left it on a chair on the bandstand, intending to replace it in its case when he returned. Then whoever did hit you either used the trumpet to throw suspicion on Buddy, or, more probably, used it because it happened to be the handiest weapon. The other instruments are all in their cases. And a gun would have been heard in the lounge, so he wouldn't use that, thank goodness!"

Jack paused, trying to get the picture straight in his mind.

"Tell me, Lee," he said presently, "who went to the kitchen with Buddy?"

Lee bit her lower lip reflectively. "Si went, I know. He wasn't hungry, but he said he was going to torture himself by watching Buddy eat, as a penance for his sins—something like that. Ray went along, too, and so did Frankie. That's all."

"Leaving Max, Jimmy, Iggy and Windy in the lounge," Jack checked them off. "Now how long before you went for your jacket did the boys leave?"

"I was going to leave with them, but I stopped to ask Max something about Kitty. So I must have left just a few minutes after them."

"Which means that any of them could have made some excuse to remain behind the others. Then, knowing that you were coming out shortly, he could have crouched behind the music stands on the bandstand, and when you came out, let you have it with whatever was at hand, which happened to be Buddy's trumpet. That's the only way it could have happened—unless someone in the lounge followed you out. But Windy will know about that, since I asked him to keep an eye on the boys."

Lee's face assumed a troubled expression. She clutched tensely at Jack's hand, and said:

"You think it was one of the four who left before me, don't you? Ray, or Buddy, or Frankie, or Si . . ."

Jack nodded in confirmation, his eyes steely blue.

"But what do any of those boys have against me? No one would try to murder me for no reason whatsoever! Or did he? Oh, Jack, I'm so frightened. It sounds mad, insane, somehow . . ."

Jack looked at her with sympathy. He was afraid too, horribly afraid. Something fiendish was going on, and he was so incompetent to cope with it, so damned useless! The same person must be behind it all. Yet it was fantastic to think that this Mr. X could commit two crimes and attempt a third without leaving some trace of his identity. Or it was possible that he had left a trace, and was now trying frantically to cover it up. Would that explain the attempt on Lee? Did she know something that jeopardized the murderer?

"Lee," Jack said suddenly, "is there anything you know about any of the boys in the band that might be of importance? If there is, you'd better tell me now."

Lee shook her head listlessly in denial. "I don't."

"But you must, don't you see? You must know something dangerous to the murderer, something that would give us a clue to his identity, perhaps. That's the reason for his attack on you, I think Tony was killed because he knew too much, too. Think, Lee, you must!"

"I have thought about it," Lee said with a hopeless sigh. "But it's all a blank to me. I knew about Iggy's song, of course. But they all knew about it. And I knew that Tony had been selling reefers to the band, but that's common knowledge too. Frankie still smokes them when he can get them."

"I suspected as much about him," Jack said. "At first I thought it might give him a motive for Tony's murder. Tony might have refused to sell him any more. But after all, reefers are easy enough to get for anyone who wants them, unfortunately. So that motive is out as far as Frankie is concerned, and I have no idea of any other motive he may have had."

"Frankie isn't as much of a crackpot as he seems to be," Lee spoke up loyally. "He's really a swell kid. It's just since Tony started him off on the marijuana that he's been getting so queer and nervous. I'm *glad* Tony is dead!" she burst out.

"There doesn't seem to be too much mourning for Andy either," Jack said gloomily.

"You know, Jack," Lee continued thoughtfully, "you can't help knowing what the boys in the band are like when you've been with them for three months, day in and day out, the way I've been. And of all the musicians in the band, the only one I'd have believed capable of murder, or of any crime, is—or rather—was Tony."

"Funny! That's exactly what Andy thought, or so Kitty said. He was afraid of Tony all right, except that he expected a knife in the back, not a bullet."

"But Tony is dead, too," Lee murmured wearily. "The whole thing is such a muddle!" And she buried her face in the pillow.

"One thing I do know, though," Jack announced with a firm set to his mouth. "You, young lady, are not getting out of my sight today, not until I see you safe in your room tonight with Kitty. No one is going to get a second chance at you. So whether you like it or not, you and I are going to be closer than a chest is to a mustard plaster."

"Right-o, my fine-feathered bodyguard," she laughed rather shakily. She sat up, and blinked several times, then shook her head tentatively.

"I believe your damp towel has served its purpose," she announced, removing it. Her hair was wet and matted where the towel had rested, but she looked better now.

Her fingers explored the bruise again. "The skin wasn't broken, luckily for me, so I suppose I'll recover."

"Much to someone's chagrin," Jack added, "But whose? I wish I knew!"

"Well, I suppose you'll want to get ahead with the business of finding out, eh? You can't sit around and watch me all day." And she swung her legs around to the side of the couch and stood up.

"Are you sure you feel well enough to get up?" Jack asked, hovering over her anxiously.

"You look as though you were going to cluck any minute," she laughed, looking at his earnest, freckled face. "Don't worry so much. I feel fine, really I do. Where to now?"

"Back to the lounge. We've got a lot of questions to ask. Only I think it'll be just as well if we don't let them know what happened to you. Don't mention it to anyone. We'll keep the murderer guessing. And Windy may have some information for me. Ready?" And he took her arm to support her.

"In a minute." Lee smiled, and walked over to the dresser to survey herself in the mirror. She looked ruefully at her hair.

"I look pretty bad, don't I?"

"You'll always look good to me," Jack answered seriously.

"That's very gratifying, but I should repair some of the ravages, at least. I'll feel a lot better with some fresh make-up on—helps the morale, you know—and I'll try to comb my hair as best I can. You wait outside for me while I change my stockings."

Jack hesitated.

"Go on, Jack," she insisted with a smile. "No one can get in if you stand watch right outside my door."

"Oh, all right," he agreed reluctantly. "But hurry. I don't like the idea of letting you out of my sight any longer than is absolutely necessary."

He stood by the mirror, watching her for a moment; then, on impulse, he leaned over and kissed her gently on the lips.

He walked out quickly, not daring to look back. He knew now what was meant by walking on air.

Lee, bless her, had kissed him back!

# 17

Ten minutes later, Lee and Jack entered the lounge together. Max, Iggy, and Jimmy were around the card table, playing a half-hearted game of rummy, and Windy was sprawled in an arm chair, reading the current issue of *Metronome*. When he saw them enter, Windy dropped his magazine and removed his legs from the arm of the chair.

"Pssst, Jack," he whispered, giving Lee a covert glance, "Didja find anything?"

"Not a thing," Jack answered, shaking his head. "Tell me, Windy, did either Iggy or Jimmy or Max leave the lounge right after Lee did? You can speak before her," he added, as he caught Windy's warning glance.

"Nope!" Windy said positively. "None of us left the lounge at all, except for the boys who went to get something to eat in the kitchen, and they left before Lee did. I know you told me to keep an eye on them," he continued apologetically, "but I didn't know which ones to watch. I didn't think any of them would go upstairs to disturb you, so I thought I'd stay here. I didn't do the wrong thing, did I?" he asked, peering anxiously at Jack.

"No," Jack reassured him. "I just wanted to make sure that the ones that remained behind stayed here all the time I've been gone."

"They definitely did. Why? You look kinda worried. Anything happen?"

Before Jack could reply, the door opened, and the rest of the band straggled in. Buddy was munching happily on a huge wedge of chocolate layer cake, and he looked as if he hadn't a care in the world. Jack wondered where that slight frame put all the food Buddy stuffed into it. Then he put his mind on the business at hand again, and watched each one carefully to discover any unusual reaction at the sight of Lee, now wearing her jacket, and comfortably ensconced on the couch.

Buddy winked slyly at her, and made some quip about there not being one of them in the band who was man enough to keep her warm without her having to go for a jacket. A normal reaction, for Buddy.

Frankie ignored her, his shifty eyes on the card players, while Si made directly for the whiskey bottle with a casual "Hi, Lee!" tossed over his shoulder, somewhere in her direction.

But Ray paused before her, and eyed her carefully through his thick lenses.

"What's the matter, Lee?" he asked. "You're rather pale. Don't you feel well?"

Jack held his breath, while everyone in the room turned to look at her. The color poured into her cheeks at this mass scrutiny.

"Ray is right," Iggy said, full of concern. "This has all been too much for you, Lee. Maybe you ought to lie down in your room for a while."

"Here, Lee," Si said solicitously, filling a glass with whiskey, "have a little tonic."

"No, thanks, Si. I'm all right, really I am. I just have a slight headache."

"You and me both, Sister!" Si exclaimed. "Boy, make that two Bromos," he said to no one in particular.

"Kitty kept you awake all night," Max said remorseful-ly. "I shouldn't have let you stay with her."

"I think a little fresh air won't hurt," Ray said, going to the window. "This place is perpetually full of stale air and cigarette smoke, not to mention the lethal fumes from those whiskey bottles."

He tried to pry open the tightly shut windows, but when he finally succeeded, a blast of snow and wind made him shut it again quickly. It was about noon, yet outside it was as dark and gloomy as if it were dusk. Jack, realized how dependent modern man was on his modern inventions. Without the telephone, they were marooned as if they were in another world.

Again he had that vague feeling of terror. So much had happened, and so much more might happen if help didn't come soon. He himself was helpless, so terribly helpless . . .

"I know what, Lee. I'll get you an aspirin," Frankie offered to Jack's surprise. "I saw some in Max's office," His bony, angular face looked, oddly enough, sympathetic. Perhaps Lee was right about the drummer.

As Frankie arose, Lee caught Jack's eye, and he shook his head with an almost imperceptible motion.

"Don't bother, Frankie," she refused hastily, with heightened color. "I can't stand aspirin."

"Oh, all right, if you don't want any."

"Please, boys, don't fuss so over me," she pleaded, look-ing distressed. "I do wish you'd forget about me and go right ahead with what you were doing. There's nothing wrong with me that a good night's rest won't remedy."

They took her at her word then, and turned their at-tention to other things. Jack sat back in the armchair that Windy had vacated, and sighed with relief. He didn't like all this solicitude. For all he knew, someone was going to try to pull a fast one right under his nose. So Lee wasn't going to accept anything edible from anyone present, not even aspirin. No sense in taking chances, because if one attempt had been made, another would probably follow, and this time, Mr. X might succeed.

What to do now? How could he ask questions about their individual whereabouts during the attack on Lee without putting the murderer on his guard?

The three rummy players settled back to their game, but Jimmy soon decided that he had had enough, so Frankie took his place. Buddy, finishing the last crumb of his cake, kibitzed behind Iggy, watching the deal.

Jimmy rose, and started a discussion with Si on Tschaikowsky's piano concerto.

"Say, boys," Buddy interrupted them, "did you hear that ASCAP* is thinking of inviting Tschaikowsky to join? And with all the hits he's been turning out lately, they ought to assign him an AA rating," Buddy grinned his wide, merry grin as he brushed off the crumbs from his navy sweater.

"Tschaikowsky is dead, you dope!" Frankie announced with withering scorn.

"No!" Buddy registered exaggerated shock, then grief. "Why, that's terrible! Simply terrible! I didn't know, but then I haven't been reading the papers lately."

Frankie sighed with disgust, and was about to go into detail, but Iggy interrupted him with: "Don't listen to him, Frankie. He's just trying to get your goat." And he flung down his cards, saying: "I'm through for now, boys," arose, and stretched lazily.

"You're right, though, Buddy," he said after a wide-mouthed yawn. "It is a shame that modern American music has stooped to rewriting so many of the classics."

"And what's wrong with the classics?" Frankie asked belligerently.

* The American Society of Composers, Authors, and Publishers.

"I didn't say there was anything wrong with them. On the contrary, I meant that making corny ballads out of music like Tschaikowsky's doesn't do his music any good, and it certainly doesn't benefit jazz in any way. So why permit it? They have no right to do it! Oh, I know that technically and legally speaking it's permissible, but they haven't the moral right!"

"Why not?" asked Ray, placidly settling back in an arm chair, ready to enjoy a stimulating discussion. He removed his glasses, and began polishing them carefully with his handkerchief as he spoke. "Don't forget that Liszt, to mention one instance, rewrote a great deal of music, Schubert's notably. He arranged it, and no one has condemned him for that."

"Ah, but your comparison isn't a parallel one," Iggy pounced triumphantly on Ray. "When Liszt rearranged a composition, he *added* to it, elaborated on the theme, for instance, or added a beautiful cadenza. The same with other great composers, like Brahms. The Hungarian dances which he used as themes were originally folk tunes. Most great composers wrote variations on a theme taken from contemporary composers, and no one objected to that. But you must remember, it's not the rewriting of a theme that should be considered, but what's done with it. As I say, these great classical composers added to the themes they used, whereas modern arrangers detract from what they rearrange. They take a beautiful theme, harmonize it with a few barber shop chords, add sappy lyrics, and then have it played in straight cut time. What kind of contribution is that to music?"

"Who pretends that it's supposed to be a contribution?" Jimmy asked. The trumpeter looked more normal now, and relieved of his previous burden. "It's just supposed to be a pot-boiler. All musicians, even your great ones, wrote pot-boilers at one time or another."

"Let Tin Pan Alley make up their own pot-boilers then!" Iggy snapped. "There's plenty of crappy modern ballads that they can rewrite, and some of them can use rewriting, believe me!"

"I recently read an article which defended the practice," Si contributed, coddling a highball. "The author's argument was that reducing a complicated composition to its simplest form helped ordinary people unversed in music to notice its beauty. And so it might encourage them to listen to the composition in its original form, once they were familiar with the melody."

"Very nice!" Iggy said scornfully, leaning against the spinet piano. "So because a bunch of lowbrows don't understand or enjoy the paintings of Da Vinci or Michelangelo, we should have a commercial artist reduce the *Mona Lisa* or *The Last Judgment* to a comic strip, and say to the lazy minded populace: 'There, now, isn't that pretty? Now you really must come and view the originals. They're much prettier, and you'll learn eventually to love them!' Hah!" Iggy's black eyes snapped with the force of his enthusiastic denunciation.

To Jack's amazement, Ray laughed aloud at this. Laughter from solemn Ray was somehow incongruous, but it certainly improved his looks. His face lost its sharp, cold look and assumed a warm, friendly cast. His mouth turned up at the corners, and his eyebrows forsook their superior lift. It was a shame he didn't laugh more often.

"You can say that again!" the first saxophonist agreed as he laughed. "Those jitterbugs don't even know when such music has been rewritten. And if, by some remote chance, they happened to hear the original, they'd think it was just a super-deluxe orchestration of the song without a vocal. The trouble with people today is that they're lazy, too lazy to think for themselves. They want everything predigested for them. So they don't want to waste any of their precious energy to listen to music actively. Listening passively isn't enough."

"Right!" Iggy's handsome face glowed at this unexpected support. "Of course, swinging the classics can't hurt them in the long run. They'll survive, just as they have till now. The reason I'm so against the practice is that it throws the classicists off us, just when they were beginning to forget the humble and shady origin of jazz. Now they think we lack material of our own, so it prevents intelligent, thinking people from listening to our music and judging it on its own merits. Hearing something beautiful desecrated so that a couple of hack writers can collect royalties without working for them is enough to turn anyone's stomach!"

"And how!" agreed Buddy enthusiastically, gazing at Iggy with open adoration.

"We have plenty of our own potentially great composers working right now," Iggy continued with a warm smile for the young trumpeter. "But, of course, it takes time for them to get the appreciation and recognition they deserve. Then, just as with the classical composers, it's very often too late. Take Bix Beiderbecke, for instance, who died so prematurely. He's known primarily as one of the great horn players of all time, and also for being an excellent pianist. But we lost a great writer in him too. Some of the fragments he left are—" Iggy searched impatiently for the right word.

"Solid murder!" Buddy contributed, enthusiastically helpful.

Frankie blanched at the unfortunate expression. His narrow-chested figure, emphasized by the tight, crew neck sweater he had donned, seemed to shrink under its significant impact, and he muttered something unintelligible under his breath.

The atmosphere of comradeship and easy discussion was shattered into a million fragments as they were all brought back to the painful present. Even Max, who had been dozing peacefully during this interchange of ideas, opened his eyes and said: "Huh?" at the tension.

Jack sighed as he was aroused from his absorbed interest in the conversation. So this was what musicians did in their spare time—talked about music. All very fascinating, but where did that get him? No place, in a hurry! It hadn't been so urgent before, but now that Lee was in danger, it was time for him to buckle down and make sense out of this mess.

Ray, once more cold and reserved, walked over to the table where the music manuscripts from the music racks outside had been gathered, and began sorting them methodically, preparatory to filing them away. Windy arose and joined him, helping with the sorting process.

Jack rubbed his forehead in despair. Think, you fool, think! he admonished himself impatiently. Perhaps if he lay back and let thoughts flow into his mind— He closed his eyes, and immediately the dreadful picture of Lee lying unconscious on the floor intruded. Terror clutched once more at his heartstrings, and he opened his eyes quickly, wiping his damp forehead.

Damn! He just couldn't concentrate. He was too much on edge. Besides, there was an uncomfortable wad annoying him in the small of his back. He put an exploring hand behind him. It was that copy of *Metronome* that Windy had been reading.

He picked it up, and thumbed through it indifferently. He came on a picture of Tommy Dorsey wishing everyone a Happy New Year. Hm! It was only the beginning of December, yet the January magazines were already out of date! *P M* came out in the morning, tomorrow's newspaper came out tonight, and *The Saturday Evening Post* came out on Tuesdays!

What a world! he thought as he continued turning the pages of the magazine listlessly. The headlines of several items caught his half-seeing eyes:

> ". . . Harry James Begins Tour of the Midwest . . . Woody Herman Enters Paramount for Four Week Engagement . . . Glen Miller Goes Into Hotel Pennsylvania for Six Months Stay . . . J. C. Higginbotham at Cafe Society Downtown . . . Andy Parker Finishing in Jersey Nite Spot. . . ."

Jack pursued the last item with more interest:

> "Andy Parker, whose successful waxing of his hit tune, *Headlined in My Heart,* pushed his band to the top again, is now in his last month at the Log House Casino in New Jersey where—"

"Last month" was right! Andy'd never play anywhere again! Jack tossed the magazine down on the table beside him. That record hadn't brought Andy such good luck.

That reminded him—he had meant to listen to that record. He had been on his way to get it when they had discovered Tony in the lounge. There was something about it that he had tried to recall last night. He tried to make his mind receptive, to relax, but nothing happened. Weren't you supposed to remember those things when you dreamed? Oh, well, maybe it would come to him later.

"Oh, listen," he said, suddenly breaking into the discussion which Iggy had started again on Bix Beiderbecke, "where—"

"Damn!" interrupted Buddy, wrinkling his nose with disgust. "Here comes Professor Quiz with those questions again. Why don't you get yourself a sponsor, and stop bothering us?"

"Sorry to disappoint you, Buddy," Jack said with a smile. "I just wanted to know if there was a record of *Headlined in My Heart* around, and if any of you minded my playing it."

"It's in the cabinet, second shelf," Ray said.

"What do you want that for?" Frankie asked suspiciously.

"I thought it might give me an idea about what happened last night while we were playing that arrangement," Jack answered as he looked through the records in the second shelf. Ah, there it was. "Don't mind me, boys; just go ahead with what you were doing."

As he put the record on the electric record player, Iggy watched him with a grim look. He evidently didn't like being reminded of that song. Jack changed the needle on the arm and clicked the switch. Once again, Andy Parker's orchestra moved into the introductory strains of the song.

The atmosphere of the room became tense again, with a tension that was but thinly disguised by the ordinary movements of its occupants. Every single person who had been on the bandstand last night when Andy was murdered was now in this room listening. . . .

What was the murderer thinking?

The few bars of the introduction came to an end, and now, uncannily, Andy came in on the upbeat with the lyrics.

How strange it was—Andy was lying dead upstairs, and here was his voice, living on after him. Tony, too, was dead, but right now he was playing with the orchestra, playing that tenor sax from the other world . . .

The room was quiet now, silent of all its usual rustlings. Iggy was sitting moodily by Lee's side, and she had leaned back against the couch, her face averted, so that only her lovely profile was visible from where Jack stood beside the record player. Ray, Windy and Jimmy stood together now, all three with cigarettes between their fingers, the smoke wisping up lazily. Even Buddy was sitting quietly, listening to the music filling the room.

Only Si was unconcerned. He had his guitar on his knee, and was polishing its shiny, ornamental surface with his handkerchief. He could afford to be nonchalant. He hadn't been on the bandstand last night . . . He hadn't heard Andy singing for the last time . . .

Which one . . . ? Which one knew the answers to the questions in everyone's mind? Which one . . . ? The question drummed ceaselessly through Jack's brain, with a tormenting persistency. Which one . . . ?

Everything that had happened was part of a pattern. Like a jigsaw puzzle, to use an ancient simile. But you had to have all the pieces for it to make sense.

Then again it was like an orchestration, every part incomprehensible, meaningless, until all the parts were read or played together; and then the music sounded right, complete. But which parts were missing? Or had he been too stupid to recognize a part when it was played?

Jack scoffed at his fancies, and listened again with concentration to the record.

Andy was moving into the release now . . . He was approaching that moment that had proved fatal to him . . . Jack found himself breathing faster. It was as if they had all been transported back in time, and the orchestra were really playing, Andy really singing . . .

Everyone in the lounge had become part of a single entity, breathing monstrously together, waiting—waiting—

There it was—Andy was finishing the release . . . He was holding the word "dreams," and there were the saxes, scurrying up—up—up—fluidly sweet. They sounded different now, fuller, and rounder-toned . . . It seemed as if they would never stop their upward climb in those swift triplets.

A bell sounded in his brain. Something was in his mind struggling for expression. There it was again, that elusive flash of omniscience. Jack tried hard to grasp it, to pin it down. He was becoming exasperated with his futile efforts. What on earth was wrong with that brain of his?

Andy's voice had entered the reprise, finishing the chorus:

The orchestra modulated with a crescendo into a higher key. The disc revolved on its turn-table, on and on, but Jack did not hear it. He heard instead the sharp bark of a gun; he saw again in his mind's eye the slim, broad-shouldered figure, imprisoned in the sharply defined, golden shell of the spotlight, wavering—wavering—then slowly crumpling . . .

He wrenched his mind abruptly from the vision and, lifting the arm of the machine, cut the sound of the music off ruthlessly. Then he put it down again, in one of the outer grooves this time, so that Andy's voice emerged relentlessly on the release again. Jack was entirely oblivious to Frankie's muttered: "Oh, lay off, why don't you!"

Again the saxes came to their soaring obbligato. Something had been wrong in that measure last night. But what?

Then the thing he had been trying so hard to remember popped into his head. Its significance burst upon him with the power and suddenness of an explosion. It electrified him. He looked up quickly, half believing that the others in the room had heard or felt something too.

Jack sank back against the table. Maybe it was just a pipe dream . . . He examined it from every angle. He thought back over everything that had happened. Half remembered actions, remarks, unimportant in themselves, came back unbidden to him, and they all supported his theory.

What a fool he had been! He had thought he hadn't a thing to go on, and the most important piece had been in his hands from the beginning. If only he hadn't been such a thick-headed goon—

His blood pressure rose, and his heart pounded away like mad. Wait now—easy does it. Hadn't he been taught that a theory had to explain all the facts before it became an accepted law? He checked back again.

Lee's eyes were closed. She was listening to the record, and her soft mouth showed the strain she had been through.

Perhaps Lee could help him. She had to! Lee was the only one who could verify his theory, give it the last added fillip that would make it fact . . .

Jack clicked the record player shut, and the voice and music died away in a descending glissando, ending in a bass croak. He rose quickly. He had to get Lee away from all these people. He had to ask her . . .

He turned, feeling someone's eyes on him. It was Ray, watching him through those thick glasses, his face blank and expressionless. Windy was still near him, eyeing the record player quizzically. Then he looked up and, meeting Jack's gaze, shrugged his heavy-set shoulders . . .

Jack walked over to the couch, trying hard to appear casual, and sat down beside Lee. She opened her eyes slowly and smiled wanly at him. Then, noticing his tense expression, she sat upright, looking alarmed. He touched her arm and said in a low voice:

"Let's get out of here for a minute, Lee, please. I have something important to ask you."

"Oh, Ja-ack!" she laughed with relief. "This is so sudden!"

"Please, Lee. I'm not kidding. You must listen to me! It's terribly important. Let's go to Max's office. We won't be disturbed there."

At the urgent appeal in his voice, she rose without further protest and followed him silently from the lounge. He took her arm without speaking, and guided her hastily down the steps of the bandstand, through the dim dance hall, and into Max's office, hardly seeing where he went. His mind was too full of what he had just discovered.

Lee started speaking once, a question on her lips, but she stopped again when she saw his preoccupied face.

He was worried now. Maybe he was just imagining things, reading meaning and significance where there was none.

They walked in, Lee in front of him, and he swung the door shut with his foot. The defective lock failed to click as usual, but now Jack didn't bother shutting it tightly. He was in no mood for trifles.

Lee sat down on one of the straight-backed chairs, and Jack leaned opposite her against the desk, too excited to sit down.

"What's wrong, Jack?" Lee asked, worried at his strange behavior. "Why are you so upset?"

Jack breathed hard. He felt as though he had just finished a hundred-yard dash. He hesitated a moment, almost afraid to tell Lee his solution, afraid she would think it wild—too improbable and too far-fetched.

"I think I know who Mr. X is!" he announced suddenly, taking the plunge.

"No!" Lee's eyes dilated. "Who is it? And how do you know?"

"That orchestration! I should have known before. But the thing is—you've got to help me make sure. That picture you saw in Rosanne Abbott's room—do you remember it . . . ?"

His voice trailed off vaguely, his eyes drawn to the door.

It was swinging in on its hinges, opening slowly, silently, relentlessly . . .

# 18

Lee stood up hastily as she followed the line of Jack's start-led gaze. He clenched his hand tightly over hers, waiting for the door to open.

Lee gasped when she saw who entered, but Jack had eyes only for the automatic pointed at them with deadly accuracy. It was oddly toylike, yet efficient-looking, and it seemed all the more dangerous for its smallness. That toy had killed two people, and now—now it would probably raise the quota to four. That automatic meant business . . .

Jack refused to think further in that direction and turned to ways and means of averting that possibility. He could have kicked himself for his stupidity, his inefficiency. He should have appropriated Max's revolver as a precaution against this very eventuality. Perhaps it wasn't too late, though. Perhaps if he edged backward imperceptibly he could reach the desk drawer where it lay . . .

Jack released Lee's hand gently, and started moving back slowly . . .

"Don't move!" The command came in a flat monotone, unhurried and assured, certain of being obeyed.

Jack stopped in his tracks. That revolver might just as well have been in Hollywood for all the good it was doing him now.

Those eyes— Funny he hadn't noticed them particularly before. It was hard to see them behind their glasses, but now as he stared at them through the lenses, he saw that they looked a little mad—round and light, with a fanatic gleam.

And that voice—with its dead, unfeeling quality, as if all the passion had long since evaporated. Jack thought unhappily that he had been right, but it wouldn't do him any good now. He and Lee certainly were in a tight spot.

At the reminder of Lee, his heart began pounding violently, and he moved closer to her, closer and a little in front of her, shielding her as best he could. He took her hand again, and at the feel of the slender fingers, cold now with fright, he resolved grimly to make Mr. X pay as dearly as possible before he accomplished his purpose.

The figure came in and closed the door with his hand behind him, his eyes never wavering from the pair before him. So he was oblivious to the fact that the door had failed to click shut. Jack's heart gave an exultant leap. The door, as usual, had remained slightly open. He tried hard to keep his eyes from fastening on the door, to keep from giving it away. If someone should happen to pass Max's office now, and happen to hear something suspicious— If! Oh, it was no use! What could anyone do against a murder-mad maniac with a gun? It was up to Jack alone.

"So!" the voice said, mocking in its very calm. "So you know who killed Andy, do you, Mr. Coler?"

"Yes, I know!" Jack spoke up boldly and loudly. "I know now. And that automatic in your hand proves I was right."

"You were right, unfortunately for you. You should have cultivated a poker face. When you sat there listening to that record, your face gave you away. But you won't have the chance to do anything about it now. Incidentally, I must thank you for secluding yourselves so conveniently for me. It makes everything so much easier." The taunting voice trailed away, and the gun pointed sharply at Lee. He was aiming . . .

"Wait! Don't shoot!" Jack commanded desperately, throwing himself in front of her. "What have you to gain by killing us? You'll never get away with it. Why, it's mass murder! It's insane! Someone will be sure to hear the shots, and you'll be caught red-handed."

"I don't think so. After I've shot both of you, I'll wipe the gun free of my fingerprints—so— Then I'll put it in Lee's hand. After which, I'll call the others, and show them the murderess who, fearing that our clever detective was too hot on her trail, lured him into Max's office and shot him. Then she committed suicide, unable to go on. The evidence will be there for all to see—a perfect confession of guilt. And the two who know about me are dead . . ."

"That gun—the police'll be able to trace it!" Jack shouted, even while he thought that it would do them a lot of good by that time—like hell! "You'll never get away with it!" he repeated.

"Maybe not," the answer came dispassionately, "but it's worth trying. As for the gun—well, you are naive! There are ways of making the ownership of a gun untraceable. Besides, what have I got to lose? I don't care much about living anyway. Everything worthwhile in life is gone for me. And this is a rotten world, so I'll be doing you a favor removing you from it. I warned you not to mix into what wasn't your business, remember? Well, now it's too late . . ." Again that gun pointed . . .

"You have been clever," Jack played desperately for time. "So clever that I wasn't certain it was you until you came in just now. I was trying to get Lee to remember—"

". . . to remember whether it was my picture she saw in Rosanne's room. It was. Frankly, I didn't think you had it in you. You act a lot dumber than you really are," came the grudging admission. "I am Rosanne's husband, or I should say ex-husband . . .

"We were married about three years ago. Rosanne said that being married would spoil her chances for a successful career, hurt her with her fans, so she agreed to marry me if we kept it a secret. I didn't care—I'd have given her the moon if she had asked for it. Anything she did was O.K. with me, I was that crazy about her. So we had a secret little apartment that no one knew about. Hiding away with my wife didn't matter, as long as she belonged to me.

"Then the band she was singing with broke up, and she got that job with Andy. That — — wolf started making a play for her, gave her the old baloney, and she, poor kid, believed him. She didn't have a chance, thought his intentions were—what do they say?—honorable. She told Andy she was already married, so that heel told her to get a divorce, and he'd marry her. She was so blindly infatuated that she went ahead and divorced me."

Jack was listening with only half an ear. He was hoping against hope that someone would pass. And what was that queer chugging noise? It sounded like a machine gun, or maybe a couple of motorboats. Motorboats! What a fantastic thought! He must be hearing things . . .

"You—you didn't contest the divorce?" he asked loudly as the voice showed signs of stopping.

"No. Why should I? If Rosanne wanted Andy, she was welcome to him. Anything that would make her happy, anything!" Bitterness and frustration were beginning to break through that steely calm.

"Then, after she got the divorce, she woke up. Andy was tired of her by that time, and playing around with a wealthy debutante. Rosanne begged him to marry her— told him she was going to have a child—his child. But that — — — laughed. He *laughed!*" The eyes behind the glasses flamed with murderous rage. Lee trembled, and moved closer to Jack.

"Well, Andy didn't renew her contract, so she had to leave the band. He was only too glad to get rid of her by then. Rosanne was desperate, didn't know which way to turn. And she was ashamed to come back to me. So she wrote me a letter, telling me everything that had happened, and that she couldn't bear to go on living any longer.

"I was out of town, playing with a band, and I didn't get the letter for a while. When it did catch up with me, it— It was too late. Rosanne was dead!" The voice broke with grief, and the gun wavered momentarily. But at the light glance that Jack gave it, the gun steadied again.

"So you see, Andy really killed Rosanne. If he had made her happy, he would have lived. But he killed her with grief and shame, so Andy had to die! You see, don't you?" he almost pleaded. "You see that he had to die. That's the law—an eye for an eye, and a tooth for a tooth, and a life for a life! It isn't a fair exchange, Rosanne's life for that slimy worm's, but it's the best I could do. So now you know."

"What made you pick last night?" Jack asked.

"I had the gun in my pocket, ready for any opportunity. Then, when I saw him talking to Kitty, I thought for a minute that it was Rosanne, they look that much alike. And then—then everything went white. I waited until the band was playing, and I shot him . . ."

"Didn't Andy know who you were?" Jack asked quickly.

"No. Rosanne never told him who her husband was, probably because she didn't want to drag me into it. He was too much of an egotist to care about anything that didn't concern him directly, so I was able to get the job with him without his being any the wiser. That was his big mistake. But that louse didn't get what was coming to him. Dying that way was much too good for him. I'd have liked to cut him to little bits, torture him, watch him suffer, so he'd know what I've suffered . . ."

Jack shuddered inwardly at the hate burning in those eyes. The madness of that gaze was terrifying.

"And you killed Tony because he knew something?" he nerved himself to ask.

"You know everything, don't you?"

"He was sitting next to you when you shot Andy, so—"

"Tony was just as rotten as Andy, with his petty little blackmailing schemes. He approached me afterward, said he saw the flash of my gun under the flashlight of the music stand. He was the only one near enough me to see. And that rat told me I'd better pay him plenty, or else! When he told me what he knew, he signed his own death warrant. So I asked him to meet me in the lounge after the rest of you were asleep—said I'd pay him off then. He wasn't as smart as he thought he was. Sure I paid him off. I paid him off with just what a rotten, dirty blackmailer deserves—cold lead! He thought he was protected. He had a knife, and was playing around with it while we talked, thinking it would protect him. Well, he has the bullet now, and I have his knife."

"And then you socked Lee on the head with the trumpet, didn't you?" Jack asked hopelessly. What was the use of stalling for time—what could help them now?

"I had to. This morning, I saw her looking at me in a peculiar way. I knew she must have seen my picture in Rosanne's room, because when Rosanne wrote me that letter, she said she was writing it while looking at our picture, because she knew then that it was me she loved, but that it was too late—too late—" His voice broke on a half strangled sob, and strangely enough, Jack felt a sympathetic constriction around the throat.

There were unshed tears in Lee's eyes. She said gently:

"You were mistaken, though. I didn't actually recognize you then. I did see the picture, but it was just an enlargement of a candid shot, not very clear. Of course, now that you remind me about it, I can see the likeness."

"So it was just your guilty conscience that made you think Lee had recognized you," Jack interposed.

"Oh, what's the difference anyway?" The words came wearily. "The whole thing was no good from the beginning. It rolled up into something so much bigger than I expected. Like a snowball, rolling down a hill. Rosanne died, so I had to kill Andy . . .."

Jack saw the door move ever so slightly behind the menacing figure. It had moved, hadn't it? But it was still now.

Jack prayed fervently that it hadn't just been his imagination, wishful thinking on his part. He had tried to speak as loudly as possible. If only someone had overheard— But maybe a draft had moved it. His heart sank.

"Please let there be help outside," he prayed. "Please—"

". . . Then I had to kill Tony to cover Andy's murder," the voice continued, "and now I've got to kill you two, because you know everything. And I may as well get it over with, instead of talking so much . . ."

The small room turned into a madhouse. There were confused sounds, strange noises . . . It had all the qualities of a more terrifying nightmare . . .

The door had swung open sharply, hitting the man before them. Jack grabbed Lee, and bore her rapidly to the floor, shielding her with his body. Just in time, because the automatic went off with a sharp explosion that had a hideously familiar sound. The shot went wild.

And then, strangely and unaccountably, there were two more explosions, louder and sharper than the first—and all was quiet.

Jack looked up from the floor, and saw two uniformed men entering the now wide-open door, the revolvers in their hands still smoking. A mob surged in behind them.

Jack put his hand up to his head in a daze. He looked through a blur at the figure writhing in agony on the floor, still clutching the automatic in tightly clenched hands. Then, blood trickling from his mouth, he sighed gently, and became dreadfully still.

Jack looked quickly at Lee, to see if she was all right.

Lee was sitting up beside Jack, her eyes filled with horror, looking at the man so quiet on the floor. She covered her face with her hands to shut out the dreadful sight.

"Poor Windy," she sobbed. "Poor Windy!"

# 19

They were all gathered once more in the lounge. The two state troopers had taken charge, and questions were flying thick and fast.

Blunt, the older and more aggressive of the troopers, finally managed to allay the bedlam. He was a man in his late thirties, burly and heavy-set, the smart uniform setting off his broad figure to its advantage. He evidently enjoyed the importance he had suddenly acquired.

"Lucky for you two that those kids from Brooklyn were stranded here," he boomed at Lee and Jack, now sitting side by side on the couch.

"Is that how you came to be here just in time?" Jack asked incredulously.

"How else? Mental telepathy? The telephone wires have been burning up Headquarters about them. It seems their parents were getting frantic when the kids didn't show up at all. Thought sure there had been an accident, which wasn't at all improbable, especially in this weather. They wanted the police to go hunting smashed cars along the roads. We tried to get in touch with this place by phone, but it was no go. The phone company told us the wires had blown down temporarily . . ."

"Yes, but—" Jack tried to edge in a word about that, but the trooper cleared his throat pompously, and said:

"I know, young man, the wires were cut. It seems the break was near town, and the repair men were able to fix it right away. All the phones in this vicinity worked except the ones from the Log House. So Headquarters sent a patrol car out to see what had happened to the youngsters, but the car couldn't get through. The roads, especially around here, are blocked something terrific. But Reilly and I were able to make it on our motorcycles. Gosh almighty! What accidents along the road. None of them very serious, though, as far as we could see. We investigated each one, looking for the kids, but no luck. Otherwise we'da been here much sooner. So they're safe here, and have been all night, eh?"

"Motorcycles! So that's the noise I heard!" Jack exclaimed. Of course—it was the same small rapid succession of minor explosions that he had thought was a motorboat. "And I thought I was hearing things."

"Yep!" continued Blunt. "That's how it was. We walked in, and when we saw the door to that private office open—"

"That door hasn't worked right since the place was built," Max said with a sigh. Everything had happened much too quickly for him to comprehend it fully as yet. Now he sat dazed and tired.

"Luckily," Blunt said, irritable at being interrupted in the fine flow of his narration, "we stood outside a minute, listening to loud voices, and when we heard someone say: 'And you killed Tony, too,' or something like that, you can bet we listened harder. It was suspicious, to say the least.

"Well, as you know, we heard plenty! A murder confession, no less! Say, Bub, that certainly was some close shave for you and the young lady."

"You're telling me!" Jack said ruefully.

"We can't thank you enough for saving our lives," interposed Lee, flashing her lovely smile at the troopers.

"Oh, not at all, Miss," said Blunt, puffing up visibly. "Not at all! It's all in our regular line of duty."

Buddy regarded them with awe. "S'help me," he vowed solemnly, his right hand up, "I'll never make another nasty crack about Brooklyn again as long as I live. Not even if them Lovely Bums fail to come across next year."

"Well, folks, you have a little explaining to do," Blunt said, taking out a notebook and pencil. "What's been going on here?"

Jack told the story as briefly as possible, dwelling but sketchily on the two murders, and Windy's motive for both of them. He didn't like thinking of the dreadful events of the past day, any more than he could help.

Blunt listened carefully, asking just a few questions, and took notes efficiently. When Jack was done, he concluded his write-up with the name and address of everyone present.

"Whew!" he exclaimed, when the last note was down safely for future reference. "Such crazy people, these musicians!"

"And what is wrong with musicians?" asked Buddy, his wide mouth tightening belligerently as he rose. "A guy steals a second guy's wife, so Guy Number Two kills Guy Number One for revenge. Doesn't that happen to salesmen?" he continued, advancing relentlessly, and emphasizing his words by sharp taps on the chest of the unhappy Blunt, who retreated helplessly before the onslaught. "Doesn't that happen to undertakers, or florists, or grocers? Ha? Answer me that!" he commanded indignantly.

"O.K., Sonny, O.K.," said Blunt with a placating smile. "No offense meant. Don't get mad now. I—er—I'm sure musicians are very nice people. I'm—er—a fan of Guy Lombardo's myself."

He cleared his throat gruffly, and put away his notebook with a sigh of relief. "Reilly, you keep an eye on these—er—these people—I mean, on things in general. I've got to go for help with those corpses. We'll have to have an inquest on 'em of course—just a formality. Three of them—think of it!" And he shook his head with the wonder of it. The other trooper went out with him for some last-minute instructions about keeping an eye on the bodies.

The lounge was quiet again. But this time the quiet was of a different quality—peaceful, without tension or strain. A ghastly experience was over.

"Shucks!" Buddy said ruefully. "It's too bad about Windy going off his nut like that. He was hot stuff on that licorice stick—oops! pardon, Frankie—I mean on his clarinet. He was some killer-diller!"

"You mean 'chiller-diller,'" Jack said. "I don't mind admitting that I was scared stiff when he opened that door and pointed the gun our way. I was sure it was the *Funeral March* for us."

"He was stark mad," Lee said, trembling a little at the memory. "I'll never forget his eyes. Who knows how many of us Windy might have murdered? And yet—the way he was killed—just as if they were shooting a mad dog— Poor Windy." She shuddered, and Jack put his arm around her shoulders in a comforting gesture. He knew exactly how she felt.

"Who is this Windy, anyway?" Kitty asked in a piercing whisper.

"Sh, Hon, I'll tell you later," answered Butch, sitting protectively on the arm of her chair.

"Jack figured the whole thing out," Lee continued with pride. "Besides saving my life when he threw me to the floor. But I still don't know how he knew it was Windy."

"Come on," Buddy coaxed coyly. "Tell us the secret of your success, you super-duper snooper, you!"

"I hardly know where to begin," Jack hesitated.

"At the beginning," Buddy was helpful as usual.

"Windy kept throwing me clues all along," Jack said slowly. "But I was just too blind to realize it.

"First of all: Why was Windy here? That in itself should have been suspicious. He's such a well-known clarinetist—you boys remarked on that—that even Andy was glad to get him with the band. You remember that he greeted him cordially last night; that is, it was cordial for Andy. Yet Windy was willing to take a third alto sax seat, practically the lowest position in a band. Andy's was a name band, it's true, but Windy knew before he came here that it was unpleasant working for Andy. He told me so himself. And he could have had a much better job. He told me, when we were driving up, that Glenn Miller had offered him a chair with the band through the agency. He slipped up there when he mentioned it, and he realized he did, so he tried to cover up by saying that he didn't accept the offer because Glenn Miller was going on the road, and he—Windy—didn't feel up to taking on those one night stands. That, of course, was an out-and-out lie, only I didn't know it at the time."

"Yeah," Frankie confirmed. "Glenn Miller just started a six months hotel stretch in town."

"Right," nodded Jack. "So I just read in that copy of *Metronome,* only it didn't penetrate at the time,"

He paused, remembering Windy's words in the car: *Music Agents offered me my choice of a berth with Glenn Miller or this job with Andy Parker. I tossed a coin, and Andy won—or maybe he lost, defending on how you look at it . . .*

"Well?" Jimmy said impatiently. "Go on, Jack."

"Oh, yes. Windy also told me that he'd been loafing, out of work for a couple of months, waiting for a decent job to turn up. Sure he was waiting—for a spot in Andy's band. Knowing how Andy's men quit on him periodically,

Windy knew it was just a question of time before there would be a vacancy in the woodwind section. He was patient, with the patience of insanity.

"And so, knowing that sooner or later he was going to get a crack at Andy, he prepared himself with an automatic. He brooded and brooded over the wrong Andy had done Rosanne, building up to a crescendo of revenge. That constant hate poisoned his mind irreparably. He kept the gun in his pocket, ready to use it at a moment's notice. Then last night, when Andy ordered the lights out for his solo number, Windy got his opportunity, also the impetus. Kitty, here, resembled his wife, and seeing Andy talking to Kitty just before he started his number made Windy's mind crack under the strain. So he shot Andy during that song. Otherwise he might have waited until he got Andy alone."

"But—" Iggy interrupted with a puzzled line on his forehead.

"I know what you're thinking," Jack said hastily, "but let me tell it in my own way. To continue, Tony happened to see the flash of Windy's automatic. Or so he said. Of all the musicians in the band, he was in the best position to have seen something. And, being Tony, he tried a little more blackmail."

"That—that rat!" Jimmy muttered feelingly.

"But," continued Jack, "Windy wasn't having any, so he made an appointment with Tony to meet down in the lounge after we were asleep last night. I guess he promised to give him some money then, and that was the end of Tony!

"Lee had told me about visiting Rosanne in her room before Andy's former vocalist committed suicide. I happened to mention it to Windy. He pretended that he was entirely unfamiliar with the name of Rosanne Abbott. That was curious, so curious that it made me wonder a little at the time. After all, Rosanne had made quite a name for herself as Andy's vocalist. Any jitterbug can tell you the name and pedigree of every member of a name band, including its singers, so it was strange that someone in the business like Windy hadn't heard of her. Yet he knew enough about Andy to inform me that he was poison to women. Windy denied knowing of her because he was afraid to trust himself to speak of her at all. Also so that no one would suspect any connection between them. Leaning over so far backward was another slip on his part, but I still wasn't suspicious of him.

"But by this time, he was getting frightened and careless. He was afraid that Lee had discovered he was Rosanne's husband, which would have given the whole show away. So when Lee went out for her jacket this morning, he slipped out after her, took whatever weapon was at hand—it happened to be your trumpet, Buddy—and tried to kill her with it."

The occupants of the lounge all looked amazed and shocked. This was the first they had heard of the attempt on Lee.

"Windy hit Lee with *my* trumpet?" Buddy asked incredulously. "I used to think I could knock 'em dead with my playing, but that guy didn't have to be so literal with my horn!"

"So that's why you didn't look so well before, Lee," Ray said.

"I was a little suspicious of you when you noticed it so quickly," Jack commented. "No one else did."

"Oh, I'll break down and admit that I have wonderful powers of observation," Ray answered with a smile. "Besides, if I'd been the one responsible, I'd have been the last one to mention it."

"That's right, I suppose," Jack admitted. "Well, Windy didn't wait to see if he had killed Lee, but went right back into the lounge, counting on the fact that Iggy, Jimmy and Max were too busy playing cards to have noticed that he'd left for a moment, in case anyone asked about it."

"I didn't notice," Iggy confirmed. "If you had asked me, I would have said that Windy was with us in the room reading all the time."

"Me, too," Jimmy chimed in.

"Of such stuff are alibis made," Jack said. "When I asked him if any of you had left the room, he naturally denied it, thinking it would throw suspicion on one of the boys who had left for the kitchen.

"Meanwhile, I had been wondering about Rosanne's husband. There seemed to be a swell motive there, if the husband had been around, but none of the boys in the band filled the bill. You've all been with the band at least six months, and Lee was the last addition to the band, except for Windy and me, so she would have recognized one of you as being the face in the picture. But she said the face was totally unfamiliar when she saw it. And yet I remember now that when you met Windy, Lee, you said he looked familiar."

"He did," Lee confirmed. "But I never connected him with that picture,"

"I didn't connect Windy with Rosanne either," said Jack, "because when Andy met Windy, he showed no sign of recognition. I thought Andy would surely have known who Rosanne's husband was—if not what he looked like, at least his name. That's why I didn't suspect Windy until the end. Rosanne had insisted on keeping their marriage a secret."

"But Windy was your roommate," Ray spoke up. "Didn't you see him leave or return when he went down to meet Tony?"

"No," Jack admitted. "I sleep fairly soundly all the time, especially after that long ride in from town. Windy undressed when I did, and to all intents and purposes went to sleep. If I had awakened when he left he could have made some excuse."

"And he's the one who said you had experience as a detective, and proposed that you take charge," Ray protested. "That was stupid."

"Not so stupid," Jack smiled wryly, "You see, Windy knew the extent of my experience was practically nil. And he thought I was stupid enough to take him at his face value. And I was, till now. He kept telling me that this mess wasn't my business or his. You see, I thought it had to be one of you, because you all seemed to have something against Andy. Windy counted on the fact that he didn't appear to have any connection with you. Then, too, he knew his way around the place. He told me he'd played in the Casino with another band."

"Yeah, for six months last year," Max said.

"So he was able to locate all the telephone wires without wasting time. The longer he kept the police off, the better for him." Jack concluded with a sigh:

"And so you see, I really should have known before, but I was busy looking for tangible clues, torn letters. . . ."

"Like my check," Jimmy smiled sheepishly.

"I did suspect you, Jimmy," Jack admitted. "You can't blame me, either. You had motive enough, but you didn't seem to have the requisite nerve."

"Thanks," Jimmy said dubiously.

"Besides which, we overheard Tony say he knew who the murderer was when he was talking to you, and he certainly wouldn't have talked that way if it had been you."

"But you still haven't told us how you knew Windy was the murderer," Iggy said impatiently. "I know it had something to do with that record. You should have seen your face light up . . ."

"Windy was right about my not having a poker face," Jack said. "Do you know—for a moment there, I thought of telling Windy that I knew he was the murderer. I thought I'd give him a chance to escape or something. I know it was a crazy idea, but I felt kind of sorry for him. But I wanted Lee to verify my solution first, and so—"

"Jack!" Iggy exclaimed warningly.

"All right, all right. About the solution: It's all very simple. I had eliminated Max because I discovered that Kitty really was going west to college this term, so Max's motive was weakened. Lee's contract was up in nine months, and that's not so long to wait for a break, so I eliminated her, also on the basis of a weak motive. That left the members of the band, the ones who were on the bandstand when Andy was killed. Everyone had a part in the arrangement to play, except for that one beat rest just before the shot was heard. That one beat wasn't time enough for the murderer to take out a gun and aim it at Andy, who was moving around at the mike. That point bothered me until I nearly went mad trying to figure it out, because it seemed to me that I had heard all the instruments playing during that crucial measure before the rest. Si was upstairs, which eliminated the guitar part, and Andy was singing, so no trombone was playing. I heard the drums, and the two trumpets playing in harmony, and I heard the piano part. I heard the saxes—that is, I thought I heard the sax trio. I like the obbligato in that arrangement, and I listened to it closely. My bass part is easy enough to play without concentrating during that vocal. Then, this morning, when I listened to the record, I remembered that last night the sax trio had seemed empty. I thought then that it was because the dance hall was empty. But I was wrong—the saxes sounded empty because one part was missing. In other words, one sax was not playing in that obbligato!

"When I realized that, I knew immediately that the only one of the band who could have killed Andy was Windy. It couldn't have been Ray, because the first sax part has the melody, and the melody missing would stand out sharper than a missing front tooth. Tony was the second sax player. The first and second saxes always play in close harmony, so if Tony's part had been missing, it would have been almost as noticeable. Besides, Tony was dead, killed obviously by the same gun and the same person that had killed Andy. No, it had to be the third saxophonist, the player of the least important part of the harmony. If I hadn't been listening so closely, it would have been almost unnoticeable, particularly in a fast triplet run. So you see, Windy had four beats in that measure, and one beat in the next—plenty of time to kill Andy, especially since *Headlined in My Heart* is played in slow blues tempo. Windy didn't have much trouble aiming at Andy, either, since he was sitting almost directly behind him.

"The rest of you probably didn't notice the fact that the arrangement didn't sound right. . . ."

"Yeah?" Frankie was indignant at this challenge to his musicianship. "We play that song every night, sometimes twice, when we broadcast it, so you don't think we listen to it any more, do you?"

"Well, it was all new to me," Jack said, "and—"

"Anyway, all's well that ends with Andy and Tony dead," Buddy interrupted, impatient of the long explanations. "Crazy or not, Windy did us all a personal favor. So let's forget the whole thing, eh?"

"What happens to us now?" Frankie asked disconsolately.

"It's back to the agency, I guess," Si said cheerfully, draining the contents of his glass.

"O.K., boys," said Buddy. "I'll meet you all in front of the Strand."

"I have a suggestion," said Ray, standing up, and looking more than ever like an owl with his solemn expression, and the long thin nose between the rims of his glasses. "Why don't we keep on with the band? All we have to do is get two additional saxophonists and a trombonist . . ."

"We need more than that for a band," Frankie said pessimistically. "Lots of money, publicity . . . It was Andy's name that made the band, and his money that kept it going in tight spots. That's a crazy idea, Ray."

"I don't think it's so crazy," Jimmy spoke up excitedly. "Andy's money can still keep the band going. It's all mine, now. We could incorporate the band, like Glen Gray's Casa Loma Orchestra. Everyone gets an equal share. How about it?"

Everyone seemed to be for it.

"I guess there's some money due Iggy from Andy's estate, though," Jimmy said rather diffidently. "I mean the royalties from your song, Iggy."

"I don't want it," Iggy said shortly. "It probably wouldn't have made so much money, anyway, if my name instead of Andy's had been on it. Put that money back in the band."

"And I guess we'll have plenty of free publicity when the reporters get hold of the story. Bet we'll be Page One!" Buddy contributed, delighted at the prospect. "Say," he said, turning his face at various angles, "which side is my best profile?"

Frankie was almost convinced. "But what about a leader? We'll need one, even if we are incorporated."

"Nincompoop!" Buddy exclaimed with infinite scorn. "There's only one person here capable of fronting a band, and that, of course, is Iggy."

"Oh, no!" Iggy was dismayed at the prospect.

"Oh, yes!" Lee said enthusiastically. "You play well enough to star in the band, Iggy, and just think, you'll be able to sell your other tunes to the publishers. Don't you see? As the leader of a big-time band you'll be a big shot, able to plug songs, and all that. The publishers will all come running to you."

Iggy considered this in silence.

"I guess I can speak for the rest of us," Ray said. "We all think you fill the bill, Iggy."

"But he gets the same cut that we do," Frankie said hastily.

"That's O.K. by me!" Iggy said, flushed with excitement. "Share and share alike. And everyone has an equal vote. You're with us, Jack? Both as bass player and arranger?"

"You bet!" Jack assented warmly. "I'll be able to experiment with a distinctive style for the band. I have some ideas I'd like to try."

"And Lee," Iggy continued. "We certainly need a good vocalist like you, and you'd be featured as a star with our outfit . . ."

"Please come in with us, Lee," Jimmy said. "You'll be a member of the corporation, same as the rest of us. If you do, you'll be making almost as much as you would with that radio commercial. How about it?"

"What a question!" Lee's eyes shone. "You couldn't get rid of me now if you tried."

"Swell!" exclaimed Jimmy. "We'll get a lawyer to draw up the papers tomorrow. Meanwhile," he continued, "we still have a job, haven't we, Max?"

"Yep," Max assented benignly, looking with a satisfied air at Kitty snuggling up to Butch. "I never had any objection to you fellers. So your band can stay till the fifteenth of next month, when the next band moves in. And you can finish out Andy's contract at the same money he was getting. That includes the network wires, too. As soon as the phone is repaired, I'll call the newspapers and change the listings in the radio columns. That'll give you some extra publicity."

"Well, I guess that settles it," Jimmy said, his new authority setting well on him.

"We'll be getting ahead with the band, all of us," said Iggy, walking up and down in his excitement. "I'll streamline the sections, make a modern combination, add two saxes, three more brasses . . . Get a good press agent . . . What's to stop us from hitting the jackpot? Theater engagements, radio contracts, a cigarette commercial. . . ." The unlimited possibilities spread before him like the promised land, and his eyes glowed at the prospect as he continued planning.

But Jack wasn't listening. He had turned to look at Lee. "I'm awfully glad you're staying with the band, Lee. That makes it just about perfect for me."

"I'm glad you'll be here too," she answered, her lashes sweeping her smooth cheek.

"You are?" he asked eagerly.

"Mm, mm. So I can keep an eye on you."

"Keep an eye on me?" he echoed.

"Of course," she smiled. "It's my band, too, now. And I have to see that our new arranger toes the mark, don't I?" Then at the look in his eyes, she flushed and added hastily:

"For the band's sake, of course!"

"Of course!" Jack agreed happily.

Print-on-demand titles available at
CoachwhipBooks.com


Ebook titles available at
Coachwhip.com

BRUTAL Question

by
OLIVER WELD BAYER
author of
"AN EYE FOR AN EYE"

*Crime*
*is of the*
*Essence*

*Joe Csida*

MURDER AT DRAKE'S ANCHORAGE

E. LEE WADDELL

MAUDE PARKER

MURDER IN JACKSON HOLE

**MURDER AT GLEN ATHOL**

NORMAN LIPPINCOTT

A strange clan—a grotesque dinner party—and violent death in a little Pennsylvania town!

*hot tip* JACK DOLPH

DEAD
WEIGHT

ADDISON
SIMMONS

DEATH
ON THE CAMPUS

ADDISON
SIMMONS

NARROW
GAUGE TO
MURDER

CAROLYN THOMAS

NOW I LAY ME
DOWN TO DIE

ELIZABETH TEBBETTS-TAYLOR

DEATH
OVER
NEWARK

ALEXANDER WILLIAMS

THE JINX
THEATRE
MURDER

ALEXANDER WILLIAMS

**LADY IN LILAC**

SUSANNAH SHANE

MURDER
IN THE
ROUGH

—

LESLIE
ALLEN

# 3 DETECTIVES
## FEMMES AUDACIEUSES
### MERWIN • SOMERVILLE • FOOTNER

# 3 DETECTIVES
## MURDER ON THE RAILS
### WHITECHURCH • THORNE • TORGERSON

THE
WINE ROOM
MURDER

STANLEY VESTAL

THE
WEEK–END
MYSTERY

ROBERT A. SIMON

THE EDINGTONS

THE HOUSE OF THE
VANISHING
GOBLETS

THE GOLDFISH
MURDERS

WILL MITCHELL

ANITA BOUTELL

DEATH BRINGS
A STORKE

CRADLED
IN FEAR

ANONYMOUS FOOTSTEPS | JOHN. M. O'CONNOR

# THE
# RUMBLE
## MURDERS

Henry Ware Eliot, Jr.

# SHOW
# BUSINESS

### A FAST-MOVING MYSTERY BY
# BRYANT FORD